Her voice was so low that it was a moment before Daniel realised what she had said. He frowned, unsure where this was leading. 'You're sorry?'

'Yes. About the way I…I've behaved recently.' She tipped back her head and looked him squarely in the eyes. 'I agreed to call a truce and I haven't kept to that. I apologise.'

'I know how difficult this situation is, Emma,' he said quietly, more touched than he cared to admit. 'I find it hard, too.'

'Do you?' She looked at him in surprise and he sighed.

'Yes. I can't just forget what happened five years ago. You meant a lot to me, Emma.'

'Did I?'

'Of course you did.' He frowned when he saw the uncertainty on her face. He had never tried to hide his feelings—how could he have done? She had meant the whole world to him and all of a sudden it seemed important she understood that.

'I cared a lot about you, Emma,' he said quickly, wishing that he didn't have to use such a milk-and-water term to describe how he'd felt. Claiming he'd *cared* barely touched on the way he had really felt about her—but what else could he say? Admitting that he had loved her with every fibre of his being wasn't what she wanted to hear. His heart ached as he repeated it with as much conviction as he dared. 'I really and truly cared about you.'

Jennifer Taylor lives in the north-west of England, in a small village surrounded by some really beautiful countryside. She has written for several different Mills & Boon® series in the past, but it wasn't until she read her first Medical™ Romance that she truly found her niche. She was so captivated by these heart-warming stories that she set out to write them herself! When she's not writing, or doing research for her latest book, Jennifer's hobbies include reading, gardening, travel, and chatting to friends both on and off-line. She is always delighted to hear from readers, so do visit her website at www.jennifer-taylor.com

Recent titles by the same author:

THE MIDWIFE'S CHRISTMAS MIRACLE
THE DOCTOR'S BABY BOMBSHELL*
THE GP'S MEANT-TO-BE BRIDE*
MARRYING THE RUNAWAY BRIDE*
THE SURGEON'S FATHERHOOD SURPRISE**

**Dalverston Weddings*
***Brides of Penhally Bay*

SMALL TOWN MARRIAGE MIRACLE

BY
JENNIFER TAYLOR

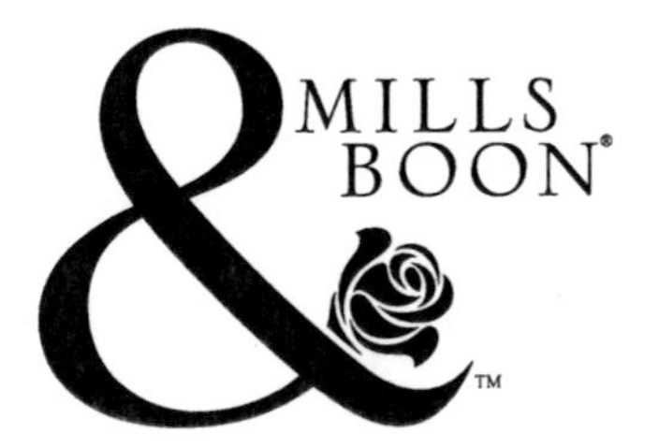

All the characters in this book have no existence outside the imagination of the author, and have no relation whatsoever to anyone bearing the same name or names. They are not even distantly inspired by any individual known or unknown to the author, and all the incidents are pure invention.

First published in Great Britain 2011
by Mills & Boon, an imprint of Harlequin (UK) Limited.
Large Print edition 2011
Harlequin (UK) Limited, Eton House,
18-24 Paradise Road, Richmond, Surrey TW9 1SR

ISBN: 978 0 263 21779 7

Harlequin (UK) policy is to use papers that are natural, renewable and recyclable products and made from wood grown in sustainable forests. The logging and manufacturing process conform to the legal environmental regulations of the country of origin.

Printed and bound in Great Britain
by CPI Antony Rowe, Chippenham, Wiltshire

SMALL TOWN MARRIAGE MIRACLE

To Pam and Dudley.
Thank you for always being there.

CHAPTER ONE

'I FEEL terrible about what's happened, Emma. You came home for a rest, not to be faced with this.'

'It doesn't matter. Really it doesn't.'

Emma Roberts smiled soothingly as she led her aunt, Margaret Haynes, over to a chair. She sat down beside her, seeing the strain that had etched deep lines onto the older woman's face. Her aunt had aged a lot since the last time Emma had seen her and she couldn't help feeling guilty. She should have realised that something was wrong and returned home sooner than this.

'Now tell me what the consultant said,' she ordered gently.

'He said that it's imperative your uncle has a coronary artery bypass done as soon as possible.

If Jim waits any longer, there will be no point doing it.'

'Wait? Do you mean that Uncle Jim has been putting off having it done?' Emma queried in surprise.

'Yes. I'm afraid he has.' Margaret Haynes sighed. 'His angina has been getting worse for some time now. Even his medication doesn't always help when he has a really bad attack. I kept nagging him to have the bypass done, but you know how stubborn he can be.'

Emma smiled. 'I do indeed. Once Uncle Jim gets an idea into his head, it's impossible to shift it.' She sobered abruptly. 'But from what you've said, it sounds as though the situation is extremely urgent now.'

'It is.' Margaret gave a little sob. 'I thought I was going to lose him yesterday. He was in such terrible pain…'

'Shh, it's OK. He's going to be fine,' Emma assured her. She put her arm around the older woman's shoulders, wishing she were as certain of the outcome as she was trying to appear. Her aunt and uncle had brought her up after her parents had died and she loved them dearly. The thought of anything happening to Uncle Jim was almost more than she could bear.

'Of course he will. I'm just being silly, aren't I?' Margaret blew her nose. 'The consultant told me that he has high hopes the operation will be a complete success, so I have to remember that and not get upset. I certainly don't want your uncle to see me weeping and wailing.'

'It's the last thing he needs,' Emma agreed, admiring her aunt's steely determination. 'Uncle Jim will need plenty of rest after he's had the operation, though. I hope he understands that.'

'Oh, I shall make sure he does,' Margaret said firmly. 'He'll be in hospital for about twelve days and after that I intend to take him away to the cottage. Jim will need at least six weeks to recover from the operation and I won't be able to keep him out of the surgery for that length of time if we're at home.'

'Which is where I come in,' Emma said quickly, stifling a small pang of regret. Maybe she had been looking forward to a much-needed rest after a gruelling six months spent working overseas, but this was an emergency. If she ran the practice while her uncle recuperated, he would be less likely to worry. It was a small price to pay for all the love her aunt and uncle had lavished on her over the years.

'I'll take charge of the surgery while you're away,' she began, but her aunt shook her head.

'Oh, no, you don't need to do that, dear. Daniel will be here, so if you could just help out if it gets really busy, that would be more than enough.'

'Daniel?' Emma repeated, somewhat at a loss.

'Yes. I'm sure I told you last night when you phoned that Daniel had agreed to step in earlier than planned… Or did I? I was so worried, you see…'

'Daniel who?' Emma put in hurriedly before her aunt could drift off at a tangent again.

'Daniel Kennedy.'

Emma swung round when a deep voice answered her question. Her green eyes widened when she saw the tall, dark-haired man who was standing behind her. Just for a moment shock stole her ability to speak as she stared at him in dismay. It had been five years since she'd last seen him, and a lot had happened during that time, yet all of a sudden it felt as though she was right back to where she had been all those years ago—madly in love with the man she wanted to spend her whole life with. The thought scared her witless.

'Hello, Emma.' Daniel smiled at her but there was a wariness about the look he gave her, Emma realised, as though he wasn't sure how she would feel about seeing him again.

He was right to wonder, too, Emma thought grimly as she rose to her feet. Maybe she *had* believed at one time that Daniel was the man for her, but she didn't believe it any longer. The truth was that Daniel had used her, slept with her and then cast her aside when he had discovered she'd been getting too serious about him. It had taken her a long time to accept what he had done, but nowadays she was under no illusions. Daniel had never truly cared about *her.* He'd only ever cared about himself.

Emma took a deep breath. Maybe she hadn't expected to see him here, but she would deal with it. She was no longer the naïve and trusting young woman she had been back then. She had grown up now and she had seen too much of the world to be dazzled by a man like Daniel Kennedy ever again!

Daniel felt as though his smile had been pasted into place. He had been dreading seeing Emma again for a number of reasons, although he wasn't about to delve into them right then. He held out his hand, playing the role of old friend to the best of his ability even though he knew it wasn't true. He and Emma had been a lot more than friends at one time.

'It's good to see you again, Emma. How are you?'

'Fine, thank you.'

She shook his hand and a frisson ran through him when he felt the coolness of her skin. Just for a moment he was reminded of all the other occasions when he had touched her. Her skin had been cool then but it had soon warmed up as he had stroked and caressed her. The memory sent a surge of heat coursing through him and he hurriedly blanked it out, knowing how foolish it was to go down that route.

'This must have come as a shock to you?'

'It has.' She glanced at her aunt and drew him aside. 'Aunt Margaret just told me that Uncle Jim has been putting off having the bypass done. Is that true?'

'Yes, it is.' Daniel sighed. 'You know how dedicated Jim is. I expect he was worried about what would happen to the practice if he took any time off.'

'That's so typical of him. He puts everyone else's needs before his own.' She gave him a hard look. 'Did you know that he was delaying having surgery?'

'No. I knew Jim had angina, of course, but he never admitted how bad things had got until last week,' Daniel answered truthfully. 'I suspect he only told me then because he needed my help. He'd finally agreed to have his op at the end of the month and he wanted me to cover for him.'

'Really?' Emma frowned. 'I don't understand why he asked you to take over the practice. He knew I was coming home, so why didn't he ask me?'

'I can't answer that. You'll have to ask Jim, although I suggest you leave it until after he's had his operation.' He shrugged when he saw her mouth tighten. It was obvious that she didn't appreciate his advice but he refused to let it deter him. 'Jim needs peace and quiet more than anything else at the moment. What he doesn't need, Emma, is for us to be conducting some sort of personal vendetta.'

'Don't flatter yourself,' she snapped back. 'The days when I cared enough to fight with you, Daniel, are long gone.'

'Good. Then it won't cause any problems if I'm in charge of the practice in your uncle's absence.'

'The only problem I have is understanding why you've agreed to do it. I mean, working in the middle of nowhere is hardly a step up the professional ladder, is it, Daniel?'

Daniel flinched when he heard the scorn in her voice. It didn't make it any easier to know that he only had himself to blame for it either. He'd been so desperate to convince her that there was no future for them that he had led her to believe that all he was interested in was his career. Now he was reaping the consequences.

'It's all good experience,' he said quietly. 'Plus,

I'm very fond of your aunt and uncle. I'm happy to help in any way I can.'

'How very altruistic of you.' She smiled but her green eyes were chilly. 'Of course a cynic would wonder if there was an ulterior motive to your generosity. Still, I'm sure the truth will come out at some stage.'

She turned away before he could reply, not that he could think of anything to say in his defence. Emma wouldn't believe him if he told her that he wasn't interested in personal advancement and never had been. All of a sudden he bitterly regretted those claims he had made about going into private practice one day, but what else could he have done? Accepted what she'd been offering him, knowing that it could ruin both their lives?

Daniel's heart was heavy as he excused himself and made his way along the corridor. There was a coffee machine at the bottom of the stairs and he fed some coins into it. It disgorged a stream of insipid-looking liquid into a plastic cup but he didn't care how it looked or tasted even. He took it over to the window and stood there staring out across the town. Avondale was a pretty little market town in the middle of the Yorkshire Dales. During the summer months, the population virtually doubled thanks to a steady influx of tourists, but at this time of the year there were few tourists willing to brave the inclement weather. He had first come to the town to do his GP training and that was how he had met Emma. She had just completed her rotations and was enjoying a well-deserved break before she took up a junior registrar's post in Scotland with a top surgical team.

Daniel knew that competition for surgical posts was always fierce, and that it was particularly hard for a woman to break into that field. Whilst most consultants paid lip service to the idea of equality between the sexes, far too many refused to accept a woman as part of their team. The old prejudices were still rife: what was the point of training a woman when she would only leave to have a family? That Emma had overcome such narrow-minded thinking and secured a prestigious post for herself proved how hard she must have worked. He was impressed. He was also deeply attracted to her.

Almost before he'd realised what was happening, Daniel had fallen in love with her and she with him. It had been a gloriously blissful time for them both until Emma had announced one day that she had changed her mind about going into surgery. She no longer wanted such a demanding career, she'd claimed. She wanted a private life, time for them, so she would stay in England and train as a GP instead. That way they could be together.

Daniel had realised immediately that he couldn't allow her to sacrifice her dreams for him. Although she might truly have believed that she was happy to give up her plans to become a surgeon, he knew how much it meant to her and that it would drive a wedge between them eventually if she didn't fulfil her goals. He had seen it happen to his own parents, watched as his mother's resentment at forsaking her career had eaten away at their marriage, and he had sworn the same thing would never happen to him.

For Emma to succeed in her chosen field, Daniel knew that she would need to focus all her attention on her training for the next few years. Even though he could have found a job in Scotland easily enough, he realised that it wasn't the answer. She would be working long hours and wouldn't have time to devote to a relationship. He would be a distraction for her, a hindrance, and he couldn't bear the thought that she might fail because of him. Although it was the hardest decision he had ever made, he decided that he had to give Emma up rather than run the risk of her ending up hating him.

He sighed as he recalled her shock when he had told her curtly that he had no intention of making a commitment at that stage in his life. He had plans for the future and they were far more important than their relationship. The contempt in her eyes as she had told him that she understood had devastated him. He had almost weakened at that point and admitted that he'd lied, but somehow he had managed to hold back. She had packed her bags and left that same night and he hadn't seen her again until today.

The sound of footsteps made him look round and he felt pain stab his heart when he saw her coming along the corridor. She must have come straight to the hospital from the airport because her clothes were crumpled after the long flight, her red-gold hair lying in tangled waves around her shoulders, but that didn't matter. She was still the most beautiful and most desirable woman he had ever seen. It was only when she drew closer that Daniel could see the lines of strain that tugged down the corners of her mouth.

He knew from what Jim Haynes had told him that she'd been working overseas for the past six months and could imagine how hard it must have been, working under the most gruelling conditions. However, he also knew that it wasn't the work or the shock of learning that her uncle was ill that made her look so drawn. It was seeing him again that was the problem. In that second Daniel realised that he had to make the situation as easy as possible for her. He couldn't bear to think that he might end up hurting her again as he had hurt her once before.

Emma took a steadying breath as she stopped in front of Daniel, but she could feel her heart racing. Seeing him again had been a shock—she had admitted that—but she could handle it. She certainly didn't intend to go to pieces just because the man she had once mistakenly thought she'd loved had reappeared in her life.

'Aunt Margaret has gone in to see Uncle Jim,' she said coolly. 'They'll be doing the bypass later today and she wants to sit with him until it's time for him to go to Theatre.'

'The sooner it's done, the better.'

There was a roughness to Daniel's voice that troubled her until she realised how stupid it was to let it worry her. Daniel Kennedy was part of her past, nothing more than a memory she had long since relegated to the darkest reaches of her mind.

'Definitely.' She glanced along the corridor, giving herself a moment to absorb that thought. When she turned to face him again, she was pleased to discover that she didn't feel a thing. 'I'm not sure how long it's going to take, but there doesn't seem any point you hanging around here.'

'It isn't a problem.' He checked his watch and shrugged. 'I don't need to get back to the surgery for another couple of hours yet, so I'll stay a bit longer.'

'There's no need. Aunt Margaret will be fine.' Emma stood up straighter, determined to get her own way. 'I'm more than capable of looking after her.'

'I'm sure you are.' He smiled, his hazel eyes skimming over her face before they came to rest on her mouth, and despite her resolve, Emma felt a little flutter of awareness in the pit of her stomach. She took a quick breath, determined that it wasn't going to grow into anything bigger. The days when one of Daniel's smiles could turn her insides to jelly were long gone!

'You always were very good at looking after other people, Emma, but you need to think about yourself for once. You've had a long journey to get here and you must be tired. Why not let me stay with your aunt while you go home and get some sleep?'

'I don't need you to tell me what to do!' she shot back, terrified by the speed of her response. One minute she'd had herself under control and the next….

She shivered as a wave of fear swept over her. She couldn't bear to think that Daniel still had an effect on her. Five years ago she would have done anything for them to be together, but he had made it clear that all he'd cared about was his career. It had been a devastating blow but it had taught her a valuable lesson: she would never make the mistake of falling in love again.

'I am not trying to tell you what to do. I'm just making a suggestion. It's entirely up to you whether you stay here or go home.'

His tone was reasonable in the extreme and she felt her face heat. She knew she was overreacting and she hated to think that Daniel might read anything into it. She didn't care about him any longer, but if she carried on this way, he would never believe that.

'I apologise. I shouldn't have jumped down your throat like that.'

He shrugged. 'It doesn't matter. It's little wonder that you're stressed after everything that's happened. All this coming on top of the journey you've had would be a lot for anyone to cope with.'

It was on the tip of her tongue to deny it until she realised that she was in danger of digging an even deeper hole for herself. Did she really want to admit that it was seeing him again that was causing her to behave so irrationally?

'Probably.' She glanced at her watch and came

to a swift decision. 'If you're happy to stay then maybe I will go back to the house. I need to unpack and get settled in.'

'It's fine by me,' he agreed equably.

'Right, that's what I'll do, then. I'll just let Aunt Margaret know what's happening first.'

'I'll come with you.' He shrugged when she glanced sharply at him. 'I'd like to see Jim before he goes down to Theatre, set his mind at rest that the practice is in safe hands. You know what a worrier he is.'

'That's true.' Emma headed back along the corridor, very conscious of the fact that Daniel was just a step behind her. She paused outside the door to the private room where her uncle had been taken and glanced at him. 'It would be best if Uncle Jim didn't have to worry about anything at the moment, so I suggest we call a truce.'

'That's fine by me.' He smiled at her and Emma felt her breath catch when she saw the warmth in his eyes. She had never expected him to look at her that way and it threw her for a moment. It was an effort to concentrate when he continued. 'I don't want to fight with you, Emma. It's the last thing I want, in fact.'

'Me too,' she replied stiffly.

'Then we'll agree to set our differences aside, shall we?'

'Yes.'

She turned away, struggling to contain the emotions that were welling up inside her. It had been months since she'd even thought about Daniel, although in the beginning the memory of what had happened had tormented her. She had kept going over everything he'd said, reliving the pain of discovering that she had meant less to him than his precious career had done. Only by immersing herself in her work had she got through that terrible period and she refused to place herself in the same position again.

She squared her shoulders. No matter what Daniel said or did, no matter how convincing he sounded, she would never trust him again.

CHAPTER TWO

BY two o'clock Emma had finished unpacking and put everything away. She looked fondly around the room that had been hers since childhood. It had changed very little over the years and she found it reassuring to see her collection of stuffed toys on top of the wardrobe and the shelves of books she'd read while she had been growing up. She had moved house several times in the past few years and although it had never bothered her, it was good to know that there was somewhere permanent she could return to.

She sighed softly as she stowed the canvas hold-all in the bottom of the wardrobe because if Uncle Jim was forced to give up the practice, there would need to be a lot of changes made. The surgery was attached to the house and it was unlikely that her aunt and uncle would want to carry on living here. Nothing was truly permanent and she had to get used to the idea, even though she hated the thought of not being able to call this place her home.

Emma closed the wardrobe door and headed downstairs to make herself a cup of tea. She glanced at the clock as she filled the kettle. Uncle Jim should be leaving Theatre soon, so she would drink her tea then go back to the hospital to keep her aunt company. It would give Daniel time to get back for evening surgery.

'I wouldn't say no to a cup of tea, if you're making one.'

As though thinking about him had somehow conjured him up, Daniel suddenly appeared. Emma looked round in surprise when she heard his voice. 'What are you doing here? I thought you were going to stay at the hospital until I got back.'

'I was, but your aunt insisted that she'd be all right by herself.' He grimaced. 'I tried to persuade her to let me stay but she wouldn't hear of it. I think she was worried in case I was late for evening surgery.'

Emma sighed. 'She's as bad as Uncle Jim. Their lives revolve around the practice and have done for years. It isn't right that it should come first, especially not at the moment.'

'It certainly isn't.' He pulled out a chair and sat down. 'They need to concentrate on making sure that Jim makes a full recovery and that's where we come in.'

Emma wasn't sure she appreciated that *we*, although she didn't correct him. She poured boiling water into the pot then went to fetch the milk out of the fridge. The days when she and Daniel had been a couple were long gone and she, for one, wouldn't wish them back again.

'So what do you suggest?' she asked, adopting a deliberately neutral tone to conceal the pain that thought had aroused, oddly enough.

'Basically, what we agreed on today. We make sure we do nothing to cause your aunt and uncle any concern.' He shrugged. 'Margaret told me that she's hoping to take Jim to their cottage on the coast while he recuperates, but he'll refuse to go if he thinks you and I are at loggerheads.'

'I can assure you that I have no intention of causing a disruption,' Emma said sharply, trying to ignore the squirmy feeling in the pit of her stomach. It was one thing to agree to a truce but it could be something entirely different to stick to it. Could they really maintain a wholly professional relationship when they had once been lovers?

The fact that she should be experiencing such doubts when she was determined not to let Daniel affect her in any way annoyed her and she glared at him. 'I said it before but obviously it didn't sink in so I'll repeat it. I don't *care* enough to fight with you, Daniel. OK?'

'Good.' He smiled calmly back at her. 'It should make life a lot simpler for all of us.'

Emma didn't say anything as she poured the tea. Daniel obviously believed her and that was all that mattered. She certainly didn't want him to suspect that she had doubts, not that she really did. She had moved on from the days when splitting up with him had left her feeling utterly devastated.

Of course it must have been easier for him to get over their break-up, she thought as she placed the cups on the table. He had never invested as much of himself into their relationship as she had done. Although he had told her at the time that he loved her, it patently hadn't been true. He would never have chosen his career over her if he'd felt even a fraction of the love she had felt for him.

She frowned. It made his decision to work in Avondale all the more difficult to understand. Taking time off to come here didn't make sense when he was so keen to pursue his ambitions. *Did* he have an ulterior motive? It was what she had accused him of earlier in the day, although she hadn't seriously believed it. Now she found herself wondering if it was true. As she knew to her cost, Daniel's career meant more to him than anything else.

Daniel wasn't sure what was going through Emma's mind, but he could tell that it wasn't anything pleasant. He bit back a sigh because he had a nasty feeling that it had something to do with him. Once again he found himself wishing that he hadn't misled her five years ago, even though he knew that he'd had no choice. He had loved her far too much to let her sacrifice her dreams for him.

'Are you still working in London?'

He looked up when she spoke, trying to control the surge his pulse gave as his eyes alighted on her face. Although he had been out with a number of extremely attractive women since they'd parted, he had never been tempted to have a long-term relationship with any of them. A few dates and that was it: *finito*. In fact, he'd gained a bit of a reputation amongst his friends as being a 'love them and leave them' kind of guy. He always laughed off the accusation by claiming that he simply hadn't met the right woman, but now he realised the truth was far more complicated. He had never met anyone who could match up to Emma.

It was an unsettling thought and he tried not to dwell on it as he answered her question. 'Yes. It's a busy practice, lots of variety, and I get on well with the rest of the team so I've not been tempted to leave.'

'And they don't mind you taking time off to work here?'

'No. They were very sympathetic, in fact,' Daniel replied, wondering what was behind her sudden interest.

'It must have caused a problem when you had to drop everything without any warning, though,' she persisted. 'Didn't you say that Uncle Jim had asked you to cover from the end of the month originally?'

'That's right. Fortunately, our practice manager was able to juggle the timetable and fit it in.' He shrugged. 'It's worked out quite well, actually. I had some leave owing, so I'm using it up.'

'Really?' Her brows rose. 'You had six whole weeks of leave stored up?'

'One of the senior partners was pregnant last summer and we couldn't get locum cover for part of her maternity leave,' he explained. 'I offered to carry my leave forward. It's lucky I did as it turns out.'

'Hmm, very lucky indeed.'

Daniel frowned when he heard the scepticism in her voice. He wasn't sure what had caused it and before he could ask, the telephone rang. He stood up before he was tempted to explain that it wasn't the first time he hadn't taken his full holiday entitlement. It always seemed like a waste of time, taking time off, when he could be working. Although he had never been driven by personal ambition, he wanted to learn all he could so he could help the people who relied on him for their care. That aim had become even more important since he and Emma had parted.

'I'll get that,' he said briskly. It wouldn't help the situation to dwell on how much his life had been influenced by what had happened between him and Emma. 'It's probably Ruth checking that there'll be a surgery tonight. Morning surgery had to be cancelled so I expect it will be busy this evening.'

'I'll give you a hand when I get back from the hospital,' Emma offered.

'That would be great.' He smiled at her, relieved that she was willing to do her bit to maintain the peace. 'Thanks.'

He went out to the hall to take the call. As he'd expected, it was the practice receptionist, Ruth Hargreaves. He assured her that surgery would go ahead as scheduled and hung up. There was no sign of Emma when he went back to the kitchen but he heard a car starting up and looked out of the window in time to see her driving away. She hadn't bothered saying goodbye but why should she? So far as Emma was concerned, she would do what had to be done and that was it. She wasn't going to suddenly want to become his best friend and he didn't blame her. He had hurt her badly and the worst thing was knowing that he could never atone for what he had done. Even if he told her the truth, and even if by some miracle she believed him, it was far too late to get back what they'd had.

The waiting room was packed when Emma got back shortly after five p.m. Aunt Margaret had decided to stay the night at the hospital so Emma had come back on her own. Ruth was on the phone when she went in, looking unusually harassed. Emma waited until the receptionist finished the call.

'Problems?'

'Oh, just the umpteenth person phoning to see if we're open.' Ruth rolled her eyes when the phone rang again the second she put down the receiver. 'That'll be another one. I'm sorely tempted to take the wretched thing off the hook!'

'I don't blame you.' Emma smiled sympathetically. 'I'm helping out tonight so you can send the next patient in to me when you get the chance.'

'Will do.'

Ruth snatched up the receiver as Emma made her way along the corridor. There were two consulting rooms and she guessed that Daniel would be using the one her uncle normally used. She made her way to the other room and switched on the light. The room hadn't been used very often since her uncle's partner had retired some years ago. Although Uncle Jim had tried to find a replacement, few doctors had been keen to relocate to the area. The younger ones thought the town too quiet to consider living there permanently, while the older ones weren't willing to cope with the difficulties of the job.

As well as caring for the townsfolk, the practice provided care for the people living on the outlying farms. Some home visits could be extremely difficult to reach, especially during the winter months. The few candidates who had applied for the post had soon lost interest when they'd discovered what the job had entailed, so in the end her uncle had given up advertising and run the surgery single-handed. However, if the number of patients in the waiting room was anything to go by, it really needed more than one doctor to run the practice.

It was something that needed thinking about in view of her uncle's health, Emma decided. However, there was no time to worry about it right then. A knock on the door heralded the arrival of her first patient, a young woman who looked vaguely familiar. Emma smiled at her.

'Please sit down. I'm Dr Roberts. I'm helping out while my uncle is in hospital.'

'Oh, I remember you!' the young woman exclaimed. 'You were in the same class at school as my sister—Cathy Martindale. Remember her?'

'Of course I do.' Emma laughed. 'No wonder you look so familiar. You're very like Cathy. How is she, by the way?'

'She's fine. She lives in Leeds now with her husband and her two little boys.'

'Tell her I was asking about her, will you?' Emma picked up the folder of notes that the girl had brought in with her. 'So, Judith, what can I do for you today?'

'It's my periods, Dr Roberts. They're so heavy and irregular that they're causing me a real problem. I also suffer the most awful pain in my tummy and lower back each time it happens.'

'I see. How long has this been going on?' Emma asked.

'About a year now. I came off the Pill eighteen months ago because my husband and I want to start a family. My periods were very erratic after I stopped taking it, but I thought everything would settle down once the drugs were out of my system. Instead, it's just got worse.'

'Have you had any other symptoms? Pain on having intercourse, perhaps?'

'Yes.' Judith blushed. 'I've never had a problem

before, but recently I dread making love with David because it's so uncomfortable.'

'Which doesn't help when you're hoping to have a baby,' Emma said sympathetically, standing up. 'I'll just check your blood pressure and then I'd like to examine you, if that's all right?'

'Oh, yes, of course it is.' Judith sounded relieved as she slipped off her coat. 'I've been putting off coming for weeks, to be honest. Dr Haynes is lovely, but I felt so embarrassed about having to explain it all to him. I couldn't believe my luck when Ruth told me I'd be seeing you tonight!'

'Good.' Emma laughed, although she couldn't help wondering how many other women were delaying making appointments because they felt uncomfortable about discussing their problems with an elderly male doctor.

She checked Judith's BP, which was fine, then asked her to undress and lie on the couch while she examined her. She gently palpated her abdomen and then performed an internal examination but could find nothing to indicate what was causing the problem. Judith had had a smear test the previous month and that had come back clear.

'And there's been no other symptoms at all?' she asked after Judith had got dressed again. 'Not even something that is apparently unrelated?'

'No…well, apart from the fact that I've had several bouts of diarrhoea. It's not something I've ever suffered from before, but it's happened a few times lately. Either that or I get constipated,' Judith added, grimacing.

'I see.' Emma frowned thoughtfully as she considered what she'd heard. 'It's possible that you're suffering from endometriosis, although I wouldn't like to make a final diagnosis without sending you for some tests first. However, the symptoms you described could point towards it being that.'

'Endometriosis?' Judith repeated. 'What's that? I've never heard of it.'

'It's when tiny pieces of the lining of the womb, the endometrium, are shed during menstruation but don't pass out of the body. Instead they travel up the Fallopian tubes into the pelvic cavity and attach themselves to the pelvic organs. They continue to respond to your menstrual cycle so each month they bleed, but because the blood can't escape, it causes cysts to form. And they're the cause of most of the pain and discomfort.'

'How weird!' Judith exclaimed. 'And you think that's what is wrong with me?'

'I think it's worth investigating further.' Emma brought up the relevant document on the computer and filled in the patient's details. She glanced at Judith. 'You need to be seen by a gynaecologist so I'll organise an appointment for you. Basically, what it means is that your pelvic cavity will need to be examined. It's done by using a laparoscope, which is a special instrument that's passed through the wall of the abdomen. There's a tiny camera on the end of it so the gynaecologist can see what's going on inside you.'

'It sounds horrible,' Judith said, shuddering.

'It'll be fine,' Emma assured her. 'And it will be worth having it done if it means we can sort out this problem you have.'

'If I do have this endometriosis, how will you treat it?'

'It depends how severe it is. Drugs can be very effective in some cases. In others, where the cysts are very large, surgery to remove them is the best option. Pregnancy can also suppress the condition.'

'So I can still have a baby?' Judith asked anxiously.

'Yes, although it's only fair to warn you that endometriosis can affect your fertility. However, let's find out if my diagnosis is correct before we worry about that.' Emma tried to sound as positive as she could but she could tell that Judith was upset by the thought that she might not have the baby she longed for.

Emma saw her out and buzzed for her next patient. The evening flew past and before she knew it, it was time to pack up for the night. She collected up the files she had used and took them into the office. Ruth looked up from the computer and smiled at her. She had worked at the practice for many years and had watched Emma growing up so there was no question of her standing on ceremony.

'I bet you're sorry you came home now, aren't you, love?'

'It did cross my mind,' Emma replied, jokingly. She held up the files. 'You'd think we should be able to do away with all this paperwork now that we have computers to help us.'

'I wish!' Ruth replied cheerfully. 'The trouble is that computers have a nasty habit of breaking down, so we need the files as back-up.'

'I suppose so.'

Emma looked round when she heard footsteps in the corridor, feeling her pulse surge when Daniel appeared in the doorway. She had been too stressed about seeing him again to take much notice earlier in the day, but all of a sudden she found herself taking stock of the changes the past few years had wrought. Although he was still extremely good looking with those craggy, very masculine features and that thick dark hair, there were lines on his face that hadn't been there five years before, an underlying sadness in his hazel eyes that surprised her. Daniel looked as though he had suffered some kind of sorrow in his life and she couldn't help wondering what had happened. Was it possible that he had fallen in love and been let down?

The thought sent a shaft of pain searing through her. Emma bit her lip to contain the cry that threatened to emerge. That Daniel might have experienced the same kind of unhappiness as she had done when they'd parted should have filled her with a certain satisfaction, but it didn't. All she felt was an overwhelming sense of grief that he might have loved some other woman more than he had loved her.

'I hope it isn't always as busy as that?' He grinned at Ruth. 'Sure you didn't ring round all the patients and ask them to call in tonight so you could put me through my paces?'

'How did you guess?' Ruth winked at Emma. 'Drat! We've been found out.'

'I…um…it looks like it.' Emma did her best to respond to the teasing comment but it wasn't easy. The thought of Daniel loving another woman was more painful than it had any right to be. She was over him and it shouldn't matter, but it did. She took a quick breath to control the pain when she saw him look at her in surprise. 'We're only joking, Daniel.'

'That's good to hear.' He smiled coolly. 'I'd hate to think you had it in for me, Emma.'

Emma flushed when she heard the irony in his voice. She turned away, busying herself with placing the files she'd used in the tray. By the time Daniel added his, it was brimming over. 'Do you want me to put these away so you can have a clear run in the morning?' she offered.

'There's no need. Dr Haynes took on a part-time receptionist at Christmas,' Ruth explained. 'There was some sort of wretched tummy bug doing the rounds and I was snowed under with all the extra paperwork. Claire comes in three mornings a week and helps with the filing, et cetera. We'll soon get everything sorted out between us.'

'Oh, right. That's fine.' Emma placed the referral letter she'd printed in the tray for posting. 'There's just the one letter that needs sending as well.'

'And I've got another one here.'

Daniel leant past her and dropped his letter on top of hers. Emma tried not to flinch when his shoulder brushed against her but he must have felt the small involuntary jerk she gave. He stepped back, his face betraying very little as he told Ruth that he would lock up and set the alarm.

Emma took it as her cue to leave. She murmured a general goodbye and hurriedly left. Although the surgery was attached to the house, it was completely self-contained and she had to walk round to the front door to let herself in. She hung her coat in the hall then made her way to the sitting room to turn on the gas fire. Although the central heating was switched on, the house still felt chilly.

She sighed. It probably felt chilly because her body hadn't adjusted to the change in temperature yet. When she'd left South Africa early that morning the temperature had been in the high 30s, so it was bound to be a shock to her system to be plunged back into the tail end of a British winter. Still, she would soon adapt…

Emma looked round in surprise when she heard the front door open. It slammed shut and a moment later she heard footsteps crossing the hall. Her heart was already racing when Daniel appeared, even though she had no idea what he wanted.

'Oh, good. You've got the fire going. It's a lot

colder up here than it is in London,' he observed, crossing the room to warm his hands.

'I suppose it is,' Emma agreed uncertainly. She frowned when she realised that he wasn't wearing a coat. He'd had it on earlier so why had he taken it off? A horrible suspicion started to rear its head and she stared at him in alarm. 'What are you doing here, Daniel?'

'At this precise moment, I'm trying to warm up. But give me a couple of minutes and I'll make myself useful.'

'Useful?'

'Uh-huh. I'll cook dinner tonight. It doesn't seem fair to expect you to do it after the day you've had.'

'Cook dinner?' Emma took a quick breath when she realised that she was repeating everything he said. 'Why on earth would you want to cook dinner?'

'Because we both need to eat,' he replied reasonably. He glanced at her, the light from the fire reflecting in his eyes so that she found it impossible to read his expression. 'We can work out a rota if you prefer, but tonight I'll cook.'

He straightened up and headed for the door but Emma knew that she couldn't let him leave before she found out what was going on. 'Why do we need a rota? Surely you'll be having dinner wherever you're staying? Most of the guest houses will provide an evening meal if you ask them to.'

'Your aunt hasn't told you, then?' He stopped and turned, and she could see the concern on his face. It made her feel even more alarmed.

'Told me what?' she snapped.

'That I'm staying here.'

CHAPTER THREE

'EVERYTHING happened so fast that there was no time to arrange accommodation before I left London. I was going to sort something out when I got here, but Margaret insisted that I stay at the house.'

Daniel shrugged but he could tell from the frozen expression on Emma's face that the news had come as a shock to her. 'I can't see that it will cause a problem, Emma, but if you aren't happy with the arrangement then, of course, I'll find somewhere else.'

'There's no need,' she said stiffly. 'If Aunt Margaret invited you to stay, I'm certainly not going to object.'

'Fine. If you change your mind, though, just let me know.'

Daniel managed to maintain an outward show of indifference as he left the sitting room, but he sighed as he headed for the kitchen. Emma's reaction to the news that they would be sharing the house was upsetting but what did he expect? It might have been different if her aunt and uncle had been there, but she probably didn't relish the idea of them being on their own. All he could do now was monitor the situation and find somewhere else if it looked as though it was going to create friction.

It was the logical solution, although it didn't make him feel good to know that he was *persona non grata* so far as Emma was concerned. He tried not to dwell on it as he made a start on dinner. He was just mashing the potatoes to go with the lamb chops and green beans he had cooked when Emma appeared.

'I'll set the table.'

She busied herself with place mats and cutlery, glasses for water and condiments. Daniel suspected that it was displacement activity, aimed at taking her mind off the thought of eating with him. He couldn't help feeling sad as he remembered all the other meals they had shared—impromptu picnics in the country, lunches in one of the local pubs. It hadn't mattered what they'd eaten or where because they'd always enjoyed it. Just being together had added extra zest to the food.

'Remember that meal we had at the Golden Goose?'

Emma's voice cut into his thoughts and he felt a tingle run through him. That she had been recalling the good times they'd had seemed too much of a coincidence, yet why should it be? It wasn't the first time their thoughts had been so in tune. Maybe there was still some kind of connection between them.

Daniel hurriedly quashed that thought. He couldn't allow himself to think like that; it was too dangerous. 'Not really,' he replied offhandedly.

He spooned mashed potato onto the plates,

ignoring the flicker of hurt that crossed her face. He was doing this for her sake. They couldn't go back and they couldn't go forward either. Not together. Leaving aside the fact that Emma no longer loved him, the old objections were as valid today as they had been five years ago. He knew from what Jim had told him that Emma was determined to make consultant one day. If that was to happen then he knew that she needed to remain completely focused. If she failed to achieve her goal, she would regret it just as much as she would have done if she'd given up surgery all together.

Daniel's heart was heavy as he carried the plates over to the table. Even if Emma was prepared to give them a second chance—which she wasn't!—there was no future for them. 'I hope this is all right for you. There's no gravy, I'm afraid. I've never mastered the art of making decent gravy.'

'It's fine. Thank you.'

Her tone was painfully polite and it cut him

to the quick to know that she was deliberately distancing herself from him. He didn't react, however, as he pulled out a chair and sat down because there was nothing he could do that would help. Emma sat down as well and began to eat. Apart from the faint clatter of cutlery, the room was silent and Daniel could feel the tension mounting as the minutes passed. He searched his mind for something uncontroversial to say, but all he could come up with was work. Still, it was better than nothing.

'How did you get on tonight?'

'Fine, thank you.' Emma forked a little potato into her mouth. She chewed and swallowed it then looked at him. 'How about you?'

'Oh, yes, fine. Thanks.' Daniel inwardly groaned when he heard the stilted note in his voice. This was hardly the best way to improve the atmosphere, was it? He cleared his throat and tried again. 'I was surprised by how busy it was, to be honest. I know morning surgery had to be cancelled, but even so I didn't expect that many patients to turn up. Did you?'

'No.' She scooped a little more potato onto her fork then hesitated. Daniel held his breath, hoping that she would find something else to say. If the next few weeks weren't to be an ordeal for them both, Emma needed to meet him halfway.

'To be frank, I don't know how Uncle Jim copes on his own. It was obvious from the number of people we saw tonight that it needs more than one doctor to run this practice.'

Daniel felt like punching the air in relief, but managed to control the urge. Two sentences didn't make a conversation. And they definitely didn't make up for past hurts. 'I agree. The workload is way too much for one person, especially when that person has health issues of his own,' he agreed soberly, trying to ignore the pang of guilt he felt. He had never set out to hurt her, far from it. He'd done what was necessary to safeguard her happiness and he had to remember that, even though it was hard.

'We have to find a way to make Uncle Jim understand that.' Emma sighed. 'It won't be easy, though. You know how independent he is and admitting that he needs help will be extremely difficult for him. Then there's the problem of finding someone suitable who's willing to work here. That will be another major hurdle.'

'Jim told me once that he'd not had much luck finding a replacement after his partner retired,' Daniel said quietly.

'No. There were very few applications when the post was advertised, so he wasn't exactly spoiled for choice. And the couple of candidates he interviewed changed their minds when they discovered what the job actually entailed.' She shrugged. 'It takes a certain type of person willing to go out to a call at one of the farms in the middle of winter.'

'Not many doctors are as dedicated as Jim is, but he has to face facts. He's not getting any younger. Even without this operation, he would have had to think about at least scaling back even if he doesn't intend to retire. Quite frankly, he can't go on working as hard as he's been doing.'

'We know that, but convincing Uncle Jim is another matter. The practice means everything to him,' she added worriedly.

'I know it does, Emma, but somehow we have to make him see that he needs to think about himself for a change. And about your aunt, too. She must be worried sick about him.'

'She is.' Tears welled to her eyes and she looked away.

Daniel reached out and laid his hand over hers, hating to see her looking so upset. 'We'll work something out, Emma. Promise.'

He gave her hand a gentle squeeze, his heart lifting when he felt her fingers curl around his for a moment before she pulled away. Picking up her cutlery, she started eating again and he knew that the all too brief moment of togetherness had passed. They finished the meal as it had begun, in silence. Daniel knew there was no point trying to draw her out again, even if he'd had the heart to try. Emma was deliberately shutting him out and although it hurt like hell, he understood why. She didn't trust him after what had happened and he couldn't blame her.

Emma refused both dessert and coffee. Her nerves were stretched so tightly by then that she would have been sick if she'd consumed anything else. She stacked her plate and glass in the dishwasher then went upstairs to her room. Daniel had mentioned something about watching television in the sitting room, but she had no intention of joining him. Dinner had been enough of an ordeal.

She sighed as she lay down on the narrow single bed. The thought of having to spend the next few weeks making stilted conversation wasn't appealing, but what choice did she have? If she asked Daniel to find somewhere else to live it would only arouse her aunt and uncle's suspicions that things weren't right between them. Although Aunt Margaret and Uncle Jim knew that she and Daniel had spent a lot of time together five years ago, they had no idea just how serious the relationship had been or, rather, how much it had meant to *her*. As far as the older couple were concerned, it had been nothing more than a summer romance and she didn't intend to disabuse them of that idea. She and Daniel would have to muddle through as best they could, although one thing was certain—if he tried to touch her again, she would make it clear that he was overstepping the mark.

Emma tried to ignore the tingle that shot up her arm as she recalled the warm grip of his fingers. She got up and went to the bookshelves, selecting a well-worn copy of *Black Beauty*, a childhood favourite. Curling up on the bed, she proceeded to reacquaint herself with the familiar characters. She must have drifted off to sleep at some point because the next thing she knew, the telephone was ringing.

She got up and hurried out to the landing, but Daniel had beaten her to it. He had already lifted the phone off its rest and was holding it to his ear. Emma felt her breath catch when she discovered that all he was wearing was a pair of pyjama pants resting low on his narrow hips. His chest was bare, the thick, dark hair outlining the solid strength of his pectoral muscles before it arrowed down to disappear tantalisingly beneath the waistband of his pants. It was only when he dropped the receiver back onto its rest with a clatter that she managed to drag her gaze away.

'That was Harry Groves from High Dale Farm. Apparently, his wife has gone into labour and the midwife is at another call. Harry has phoned for an ambulance but it will be at least an hour before it gets there,' Daniel explained. 'I said I'd go over there straight away.'

'High Dale Farm is right up in the hills. It's a long drive even from here, so no wonder the ambulance will need time to get there,' Emma agreed worriedly.

'Is it marked on the map?' Daniel asked, referring to the Ordnance Survey map they kept in the surgery. It showed the location of every farm in their catchment area, with the roads leading to it marked in red.

'It should be. It's certainly one of the most difficult places to find if you don't know the area.' Emma hurried back into her room and slipped on her shoes. 'I'll fetch it while you get dressed.'

'Thanks. Oh, and can you bring me a printout of Mrs Groves's most recent notes? I don't want to go unprepared.'

'Will do.'

Emma ran down the stairs. There was a set of keys for the surgery on the hook by the door and she picked them up then snatched her coat off the peg. Although it was the end of March, the air felt frosty as she made her way to the surgery and let herself in. Once she'd turned off the alarm, she found the map and checked that the farm was marked on it. She groaned as she traced her finger along the route. As she'd thought, it was one of the most difficult places to reach.

After printing out a copy of Sarah Groves's

notes, she ran back to the house. Daniel had started his car and was ready to leave by the time she got there. Emma hurried round to the passenger side and opened the door. 'Turn left as soon as we leave here, then right at the cross-roads.'

'You don't need to come, Emma. So long as I have the map, I should be able to find the place.'

Emma shook her head as she slid into the seat. 'You can't map-read and navigate these roads. They're little more than cart tracks in places.'

She fastened her seat belt, hoping that he wasn't going to argue with her as she really didn't feel like a confrontation at this time of the night. It was a relief when he put the car in gear and headed out of the drive.

'Seeing as you're here, can you read through Mrs Groves's notes,' he suggested as soon as they were on the road. 'Her husband said that it had been a textbook pregnancy so far, but I'd like to be sure. There's a torch in the glove box. You can use that instead of turning on the interior light.'

Emma nodded as she found the torch. It would make it easier for Daniel to see where he was going if he didn't have to contend with the glare from the interior lights. She shielded the end of the torch with her hand as she quickly read through the notes that had been made when Sarah Groves had last visited the surgery.

'There's nothing here to indicate a problem,' she told Daniel as they reached the crossroads and turned right. 'She was seen last week and her BP was fine. Nothing showed up in her urine sample either, and there was no sign of oedema.'

'How many weeks is she? I asked the husband but he was in such a state he couldn't remember.'

'Thirty-five,' Emma told him, checking the woman's chart.

'That's not too bad, is it? I know that technically a baby is considered premature if it's born before thirty-seven weeks, but it should be a decent enough weight by this stage.'

'I wonder why she's gone into labour. Did the husband say if she was bleeding?'

'No. I did ask him, but he was almost incoherent and didn't seem to be taking much in. He just kept asking how soon I could get there.' She felt him glance at her. 'You're wondering if there's a problem with the placenta?'

'Yes.' Emma felt a shiver run down her spine when he correctly interpreted her thoughts. Once, the fact that they'd been so much in tune had delighted her, but now it filled her with alarm. She didn't want to share that kind of closeness with him ever again.

'It's one of the causes of premature labour so we certainly can't rule it out.' He slowed down and peered through the windscreen. 'There's another junction coming up. Which way now?'

'Straight on for about ten miles then we'll need to turn off the main road and head into hills,' she told him, checking the map.

'That's when the fun really starts, is it?' he asked with a laugh as he picked up speed again.

'It will be fine.'

'Spoken like someone who's used to tearing around the back of beyond. Jim told me that you've done several stints overseas in the last couple of years. How did you get into that sort of work?'

'Richard suggested it. He worked for an aid agency when he was a junior registrar and said it was invaluable experience.'

'Richard?'

'Richard Walker, my boss,' she explained.

'You obviously get on well with him,' he observed, and she frowned when she heard the edge in his voice. She had the impression that something had displeased him, but had no idea what it could be.

'Yes, I do,' she said a shade defensively. 'All the team think very highly of him, in fact.'

'I see.' He changed gear then glanced at her and there was no sign of anything other than friendly interest on his face. 'Working overseas must be challenging, I imagine.'

'Sometimes.' She shrugged. 'It all depends where you're working. If you're based at a clinic, like the one I've just worked in, then it tends to be easier. The facilities are better, and there's usually more staff to help out than if you're working at a field hospital.'

'And do you enjoy surgery as much as you thought you would?'

Emma frowned. She had the strangest feeling that her answer was important to him and couldn't understand why. Why should it matter to Daniel if she was happy or not? He certainly hadn't cared about her happiness five years ago, had he?

The thought pierced a hole right through the protective shell she had built around her heart. It was an effort to respond when it felt as though it was in danger of cracking wide open. It was only pride that gave her the strength to carry on, pride plus a desire not to let him know how badly he had hurt her.

'Yes, I do. It's everything I hoped it would be.'

She laughed wryly. 'I suppose I should thank you, Daniel. If you hadn't been so committed to your own career, I might have turned down the chance to become a surgeon and that would have been a huge mistake. I don't doubt that in time I would have come to regret my decision.'

CHAPTER FOUR

DANIEL drew up in front of the farmhouse and switched off the engine. Emma hadn't faltered as she had directed him along a series of increasingly narrow tracks. He knew that he would have had a much harder time finding the farm without her help but, contrarily, wished that she had stayed at home. At least then he wouldn't have to face up to the realisation that he had been right all along. Their relationship would never have survived if she had given up her dreams to be with him.

'I'll let Harry know that we're here.' She got out of the car and ran over to the house. The door was open and she didn't waste time knocking before she hurried inside.

Daniel got out and took his case out of the back.

He also lifted out the pack of medical supplies that Jim kept ready for just such an emergency as this. There was no sign of Emma when he let himself into the house but he could hear voices coming from upstairs so headed in that direction and soon found himself in the main bedroom. A fair-haired man in his thirties, whom he assumed must be Harry Groves, was holding the hand of the woman lying on the bed. She was very pale and obviously in a great deal of pain. Emma was in the process of checking her pulse so Daniel left her to deal with that while he introduced himself.

'I'm Daniel Kennedy. I'm covering for Dr Haynes while he's in hospital.'

'So Emma said,' Harry replied. He looked anxiously at the door. 'Did you pass the ambulance on your way here?'

'No, but it may have taken a different route from us.' Daniel smiled reassuringly at the couple. 'Can you tell me exactly what's happened?'

'I started having pains after tea but thought it was because of the way the baby was lying,' Sarah Groves explained. 'I lay down on the settee for a while and that seemed to help, but then the pains started again, worse than ever. That's when I discovered I was bleeding. I told Harry to phone the midwife, but she was out at another call so he phoned for an ambulance.' Her voice shook. 'When they said it would take over an hour for it to get here, he rang the surgery.'

'You did exactly the right thing,' Daniel said soothingly. He glanced at Emma, hoping his feelings didn't show. Maybe it was foolish to feel upset but he couldn't help it. In a tiny corner of his heart, he had nurtured the hope that their love could have overcome any obstacle. Even though he hadn't been prepared to take that risk, it had been something to cling to, but now he could see how stupid it had been. His relationship with Emma would have ended the same way as his parents' had done if they had stayed together.

'We need to know how much longer the ambulance is going to be,' he said with a heavy heart.

'I'll get onto Ambulance Control and see if they can give us an update,' Emma offered immediately.

She left the bedroom and Daniel turned his attention to Sarah again, relieved to have something to focus on apart from his aching heart. 'Has the bleeding stopped now?'

Sarah shook her head, her pretty face clouded with worry. 'No. In fact, I think it's got worse in the last ten minutes or so.'

'I'll just take a look, if that's all right with you.'

Daniel drew back the bedding, struggling to hide his dismay when he saw the bright red pool that had collected on the sheets. He fetched the foetal stethoscope from the pack of emergency medical supplies and listened to the baby's heartbeat. It was slightly slower than it should have been but not worryingly so, which was a relief. He had just finished when Emma came back and he could tell immediately that it wasn't good news when she beckoned him over to the door.

'What's happened?' he demanded.

'Apparently, the ambulance has had a puncture. They're waiting for the breakdown truck, so Ambulance Control has dispatched a second vehicle.'

Daniel rolled his eyes. 'Which means we're starting from scratch. It could be another hour before an ambulance gets here.'

'It looks like it.' Emma looked at Sarah. 'How is she?'

'She's lost a lot of blood. I'm going to set up a drip, which should help, but I'm not happy with the way things are going.'

'How about the baby?'

'Foetal heartbeat is slightly slower than I would like it to be. We'll need to keep a close check on what's happening.'

'It looks like a placental abruption, doesn't it?'

'Yes, that's my guess too. At least part of the placenta has become detached from the wall of the uterus.' He sighed. 'If we were able to perform an ultrasound scan then we could tell how bad the abruption is, but at the moment we're batting in the dark.'

'What's going on, Doctor? I may not have seen a human baby being born before but I've delivered umpteen lambs and I know this isn't normal.'

Daniel turned when Harry came to join them. The farmer was obviously worried and Daniel led him out onto the landing. The last thing he wanted was to upset Sarah any more. 'The bleeding could be a sign that the placenta has become partially detached from the wall of the uterus.'

'But why?' Harry demanded. 'Sarah's been fit as a fiddle up to now, so why on earth should this have happened right out of the blue?'

'It's impossible to say. These things just happen sometimes and there's no explanation as to why.'

Daniel glanced back into the room. Emma was bending over the bed while she inserted a cannula into the back of Sarah's hand. Her face was set with concentration, even though she must have performed the procedure many times before. Daniel felt a wave of emotion wash over him as he watched her. He might regret having to let her go but he knew that he would do the same thing all over again. He simply couldn't bear it if Emma ended up hating him for ruining her life.

Emma could feel Daniel watching her but she didn't look up. She felt too emotionally raw to take that risk. Had Daniel ever regretted breaking up with her? she wondered as she taped the cannula into place. Had he ever missed her? Even though she knew how stupid it was, she couldn't help wishing that he'd felt *something*.

Sarah moaned softly, clutching her stomach, and Emma quickly returned her thoughts to what was going on. 'Are the pains coming at regular intervals?' she asked, placing her own hand on the woman's distended abdomen.

'I don't know...they seem to be coming closer together,' Sarah murmured.

Emma kept her hand on Sarah's abdomen and felt it tense as her uterus contracted. There was no doubt in her mind that Sarah was in labour. She reached for the foetal stethoscope and checked the baby's heartbeat, frowning when she discovered how slow it was. It was a sign that the baby was in distress and that they needed to take immediate steps to help it. She beckoned Daniel over to the bed.

'The baby's heartbeat has dropped. We need to deliver it as soon as possible.'

'A Caesarean section, you mean?'

'Yes. I know it's not ideal to do it here, but we don't have a choice,' she said, hoping he wouldn't disagree with her. 'Even if the ambulance arrives in the next few minutes, it will take at least another hour to get Sarah to hospital. That's way too long in my opinion.'

'You're right, we can't afford to wait that long.' His dark brows rose. 'It's been ages since I did my obstetrics rotation. I assisted with a couple of sections then but I've not done any since. How about you?'

'I did one a couple of weeks ago,' Emma told him.

'Great! You lead and I'll assist.'

It was all arranged with the minimum of fuss. Although it made sense for her to take the lead in view of her surgical background, Emma was a little surprised that Daniel had suggested it. It certainly didn't gel with the idea of him wanting to cover himself with glory, did it?

There was no time to dwell on the thought, however. Emma unpacked the emergency medical supplies while Daniel explained what they were going to do. Sarah and Harry were naturally concerned, but once Daniel had told them that their baby was in distress, they agreed to go ahead. In a very short time, everything was organised.

Emma draped the bed with clean sheets while Daniel attended to the anaesthetic. Harry showed her where the bathroom was so she could scrub up. Daniel did the same and then they helped each other glove up. Harry had elected to stay with his wife so once Emma had swabbed Sarah's abdomen with antiseptic solution, she set to work, knowing there was no time to lose.

Daniel handed her a scalpel, standing back as she made a horizontal incision just above the bikini line. Any qualms she may have had about carrying out the procedure soon disappeared as she focused on what needed doing. Within a very short time she was able to lift the baby out of Sarah's womb and hand it to Daniel, who wrapped it in a clean towel and carried it over to the chest of drawers that was doubling as an examination table. There was a moment when they all held their breath and then the baby cried, a tentative sound at first that soon grew louder.

'Congratulations!' Emma smiled at the couple. 'You have a lovely little boy.'

'A boy?' Harry repeated. He appeared completely shocked after what had happened and stared at her in confusion. 'We decided that we'd wait until the baby was born to find out what it was, but we were convinced we were having a little girl. Are you sure it's a boy?'

'Oh, yes, there's definitely no mistake about that. He's got all the necessary bits and pieces,' Emma replied with a laugh. She delivered the placenta and checked that there were no bits missing from it then set about stitching up the wound. Daniel brought the baby over to the bed while she was doing so.

'So who gets first go at holding him?' he asked.

'Sarah,' Harry said promptly. He bent and kissed his wife tenderly on the cheek. 'If it wasn't for Sarah, we wouldn't have this little fellow.'

Daniel placed the tiny mite in his mother's arms, smiling as he watched Sarah pull back the folds of towel to perform the age-old ritual of counting his fingers and toes. Emma looked away when she felt a lump come to her throat. Once upon a time she had imagined just such a scene, only the baby whose toes were being counted had been hers and Daniel's. That was how much she had loved him, enough to want to give him a child.

Tears stung her eyes as she busied herself, stitching up. Even though she was over him, it still hurt to recall how much she had once loved him. She had wanted the whole lot with Daniel—marriage, motherhood, years and years of happily-ever-after as a family.

Would she ever have a family now? she wondered suddenly. Ever experience the joy of holding her own child in her arms?

She tried to picture it but it was impossible to imagine a life not dictated by her work. It made her question if she was right to devote every waking minute to her job, and it was worrying to be beset by doubts. For the past five years her work had been what had kept her centred, what had given meaning to her life, but all of a sudden she found herself wanting more, a life that wasn't shaped by the demands of her profession, and it was unsettling. However, the worst thing of all was that it was being around Daniel that had triggered such thoughts.

It was an effort to push it to the back of her mind as she finished off. She made Sarah comfortable and then Daniel helped her clear everything away. By the time they'd finished, the ambulance was pulling up outside. Sarah was reluctant to leave the house at first until Emma gently explained that she and baby Thomas needed to be checked over in the hospital's maternity unit. Although little Thomas appeared to be fit and healthy, technically he was premature, and Sarah herself had lost a lot of blood: it would be foolish to take any risks at this stage.

She and Daniel waited while the family were loaded on board the ambulance then they got into the car and followed it back to the main road. It roared away, taking the opposite direction from where they were heading.

'All in all, I'd say that was a good night's work, wouldn't you?'

Daniel's voice echoed with satisfaction and nothing else. If he'd experienced even a fraction of the anguish she had felt earlier then it certainly wasn't apparent, Emma thought sickly as she murmured her agreement. Maybe they had never discussed having children but in her mind the two were linked—when you loved someone, you wanted to have a child with them. It proved beyond any doubt that Daniel's feelings for her hadn't been what he had claimed. Although she should have felt glad that she was rid of him, oddly enough it hurt to have yet more proof of the way he had lied to her.

Daniel knew that he would remember that night for a long time to come. Seeing little Thomas make his appearance in the world had touched him in a way he had not expected it to. All he'd been able to think about was how wonderful it would have been if he'd been watching his own child—his and *Emma*'s son—being born.

He glanced at her as they reached the outskirts

of the town but she wasn't looking at him. Her eyes were closed, although he didn't think she was asleep. Had she been moved by tonight's events, wondered how it would have been if it had been their child? He doubted it. Emma had made her feelings perfectly clear when she had told him that she was glad they had parted. She certainly wasn't wasting her time by thinking about what might have been!

A feeling of dejection swept over him as he drew up in front of the house. He'd known it would be difficult to see Emma again when he had agreed to run the practice, but he had never imagined that he would feel this wretched. The only way he could hope to get through the coming weeks was to forget what had happened in the past and focus on what was happening at the present moment. And the one thing that was crystal clear was that Emma had moved on.

Daniel followed her into the house and headed straight for the kitchen to make himself a cup of tea in the probably vain hope that it would give him a much-needed boost. He hadn't expected Emma to join him and looked round in surprise when he heard her follow him into the room. 'Would you like a drink as well?'

'Please. I don't know if it's the excitement of what happened tonight or the fact that all that travelling has upset my body clock, but I'm too wide awake to sleep.' She tossed her coat over a chair and went to the cupboard. 'I wonder if there's any hot chocolate… Ah, yes, there it is.'

She stood on tiptoe to try and reach the jar of drinking chocolate but it was just out of her grasp. Daniel crossed the room and lifted it down off the shelf. 'Here you go, shorty,' he said without thinking.

'I'm not short, just tidily packaged,' she retorted, as she'd done so many times when he had teased her about her height.

Daniel felt the blood rush to his head. He remembered only too well what came next, how he would apologise for the supposed slight with a kiss. His eyes flew to Emma's face and his blood pressure zoomed several more notches up the scale when he saw that she too remembered what had used to happen. Whether it was that or the fact that his emotions were already in turmoil he didn't know but all of a sudden he found himself bending towards her until he was close enough to feel the moistness of her breath cloud on his lips.

'Emma.'

He wasn't sure if he actually spoke her name out loud or not. He was beyond hearing by that point, beyond everything including reason. What did it matter if he had just resolved to forget about the past? It wasn't a sin if he changed his mind, was it? All he wanted was to feel her lips under his once more, taste their sweetness, savour their warmth and softness. One kiss was all he asked for, just one kiss to stave off the pain that was gnawing away at his heart. Surely it wasn't wrong to allow himself this one brief moment of pleasure?

His head dipped until merely a millimetre separated them. Daniel could feel the heat of her skin now, smell the scent of the soap she'd used. Memories crowded his mind but he no longer needed to recall the past when he had a chance to create a whole new delicious present…

His mouth touched hers and the shock of the contact almost brought him to his knees. He could feel the blood rushing through his veins like liquid fire, feel the heat that invaded every cell in his body, and groaned. His hands lifted as he went to draw her closer so that he could feel the soft curves of her body moulding themselves against the hardness of his, but he never got the chance. With a tiny cry of alarm, Emma pushed him away and ran from the room.

Daniel leant back against the worktop, needing its support as all the strength suddenly drained from his body. He desperately wanted to go after her but he knew it would be the wrong thing to do. Maybe he could persuade her to let him kiss her again—possibly even do more than kiss her—but it wouldn't be fair. Perhaps there was still some vestige of attraction between them, but it didn't alter the fact that he could so easily ruin her life even now. Emma needed to focus on her job now more than ever or she could end up losing everything she had worked so hard for. Nothing was worth that risk, certainly not his own selfish desires.

Emma slammed the bedroom door, scarcely able to believe what had happened. She wanted to blame Daniel for it but she was too honest to claim that she hadn't been partly at fault. She had wanted him to kiss her, wanted it so much that her cheeks burned with shame. Hadn't she learned anything from past experiences? Did she really want to find herself right back where she'd been five years ago, her life in tatters, her heart broken?

She pressed her fist against her mouth to stem the sob that threatened to escape it. She refused to cry, refused to risk her hard-won composure by breaking down. So what if she had been tempted for a moment? She had come to her senses in time, hadn't she? If anything, it proved that she could handle this situation. Daniel's kiss may have been tempting but she had realised the risks, assessed the damage it could cause, and taken steps to stop what was happening. She should be proud of herself for what she had done.

The thought steadied her. She quickly undressed and got into bed, pulling the quilt up to her chin. It was gone midnight and she needed to get some sleep if she hoped to be fit enough to help out at morning surgery…

The sound of footsteps climbing the stairs made her eyes fly open. She hadn't thought to ask Daniel which room he was using and found herself holding her breath as she waited for him to reach the landing. The house was large and there were a number of empty bedrooms, including the room next to hers.

Her breath whooshed out in relief when she heard his footsteps fade. He was obviously using the guest room, which was on the opposite side of the house. For some reason, she felt safer knowing that he wasn't sleeping in the room next to hers. She had resisted temptation once tonight and she didn't intend to put herself to the test again. She might not like the idea, but she had to face the fact that she might not have the strength to hold out a second time.

CHAPTER FIVE

'THAT'S excellent news. Thank you for letting me know... Yes, of course. I'll pass on your message.'

Daniel replaced the phone and leant back in his chair. Morning surgery had ended and he'd been getting ready to go out to some house calls when Harry Groves had phoned to tell him that Sarah and baby Thomas had been given a clean bill of health by the consultant at the hospital. Harry had asked him to pass on the news to Emma, which he would do, but he needed a few minutes' breathing space before he sought her out.

He sighed as he tipped back his chair and stared at the ceiling. The memory of what had happened the previous night had continued to haunt him. He kept remembering that kiss and how sweet it had been, even though he knew how stupid it was. He had made a mistake by kissing her and he had no intention of repeating it, so it would be better if he put it out of his mind; however, it was proving to be easier said than done. Every time his thoughts wandered, he could feel Emma's mouth under his and it was driving him mad!

'Ruth said there's quite a lot of calls to do today, so do you want me to help?'

The sound of Emma's voice almost made him tip over the chair. Daniel hurriedly returned it to all four legs as he turned towards the door. He'd made a point of leaving the house extra early that morning so it was the first time he'd seen her that day. Now he found his senses running riot as he took stock of her slender figure encased in a neat grey skirt and a crisp white blouse. It may not have been the sexiest of outfits, granted, but it definitely did something for him.

'No, it's fine.' Daniel dragged his unruly thoughts back into line again and prayed they would stay there. That sort of thinking wasn't going to help one jot. 'I imagine you want to visit your uncle this afternoon, so I'll do the calls.'

'Well, if you're sure?' She gave him a moment to reconsider then shrugged. 'I'll do them tomorrow, then. OK?'

'Fine, although don't feel that you have to. After all, Jim asked me to cover for him.'

He'd only meant to point out that she wasn't under any obligation to work in the surgery. Although he appreciated the offer, she had come home for a holiday and it seemed a shame that her plans should be scuppered. However, that obviously wasn't how she took it. Daniel's heart sank when he saw the mutinous set to her mouth.

'I'm very much aware of that, thank you. Don't worry, Daniel, I don't intend to step on your toes. So far as my aunt and uncle are concerned, you're the knight in shining armour who's come to rescue them. Let's just hope they still feel the same way in a few weeks' time.'

'Meaning what precisely?' he demanded, stung by the comment.

She shrugged. 'That I still find it hard to believe it was purely altruism that brought you here. There has to be something in it for you, personally or professionally, otherwise why would you give up so much of your free time to work in the back of beyond?'

'I see. So what do you think I'm hoping to gain from it?' he asked, refusing to let her see how much it hurt to hear her judge him so harshly. Maybe it was his own fault that she had such a low opinion of him, but if she had loved him—as she'd once claimed—surely she shouldn't have been so willing to believe the worst?

'I don't know. I haven't worked that out yet.' She gave him a cool smile. 'But when I do, you'll be the first to know.'

She left the room, leaving the door wide open. Daniel listened to the sound of her footsteps receding along the corridor and sighed. He could go after her and tell her that she was wrong, that his motives were of the very highest order, but she wouldn't believe him. She wanted to think badly of him, wanted to bury any feelings she'd had for him under a blanket of mistrust. It shouldn't be that difficult, not after what he had done. She must be ninety-nine per cent certain that he was a rat of the first order, but obviously she was keen to add that precious last one per cent to the score. And finding out that he had an ulterior motive for offering to cover for Jim would be the perfect way to round up the total, so help him.

Emma went back to the house and made herself a sandwich. She took it up to her room, unwilling to stick around in case Daniel decided to have his lunch before he did the calls. She was still smarting from their most recent confrontation and needed time to calm down before she saw him again.

She sighed as she took a bite of the bread.

It would take more than a few hours to soothe her feelings where Daniel was concerned. Every time she spoke to him, she felt so churned up inside that it was hard to maintain an outward show of composure. Maybe it was always difficult to relax with someone you'd once been heavily involved with—she really didn't know.

Although she'd been out with several different men in the last few years, she had never had a serious relationship with any of them. She had told herself that she was too busy with her career to worry about that side of her life but it wasn't true. Her experiences with Daniel had put her off, made her wary of getting involved with anyone again. However, she couldn't allow the past to continue influencing her or she would never be truly free of him. She had to put what had happened behind her. And mean it.

Emma finished her lunch, wondering if this might prove to be a turning point. Discovering that Daniel was working here had been a shock but it could turn out to be a good thing. Seeing him again had awoken a lot of feelings she'd thought were dead and now she would be able to dispatch them for ever. And if she did find out that he had his own agenda for agreeing to cover for her uncle then so much the better. It would put the final nail in the coffin of their relationship.

Daniel got through the house calls faster than he'd expected. He checked his watch after he left his final call and realised that he had time to drop into the hospital. It would only take him ten minutes or so to drive there and he would like to see how Jim was faring.

He started his car, refusing to speculate as to how Emma would feel about him joining her at her uncle's bedside. She'd made it perfectly clear yesterday that she hadn't wanted him there, but it was hard luck. He just wanted to reassure the older man that everything was going smoothly, or at least everything to do with the running of the *practice*. So far as his relationship with Emma, well, it would be better not to mention that.

He managed to find a parking space close to the main doors, which was a minor miracle. Hurrying inside, he made his way to the lift and pressed the button. It arrived promptly and he was about to step inside when he heard someone calling his name. Glancing round, he spotted Emma crossing the foyer, carrying two cardboard containers of coffee. She glared at him as she drew closer.

'What are you doing here?'

'I came to see how Jim was doing,' he replied evenly, putting out his hand to stop the lift doors closing.

'He's fine,' she said shortly, stepping inside. 'I had a word with his consultant and he's very happy with how things went.'

'That's good to hear.' Daniel stepped into the lift. Pressing the button for their floor, he turned to her. 'Your aunt must be very relieved.'

'Of course.' Her tone was clipped. 'What Uncle

Jim needs now is plenty of rest. What he doesn't need is a lot of people visiting him.'

'I agree. However, he'll be able to rest more easily once he's sure that everything is running smoothly at the surgery.'

'I've already assured him that everything is fine.' She tipped back her head, a hint of challenge in her eyes. 'It doesn't need both of us to give him a progress report, Daniel. I'm perfectly capable of doing that by myself.'

'I'm sure you are, but knowing Jim he will still worry in case you're keeping something from him.' He shrugged. 'Jim knows that I'll tell him the truth.'

'Tell the truth and shame the devil. Is that the maxim you live by, Daniel, or only when it suits you?'

'I do my best to be truthful at all times,' he said quietly.

A flash of hurt crossed her face. 'Really? Then all I can say is that there must be more than one version of the truth in your world.'

The lift came to a halt and she got out before he could reply, although what he could have said was open to question. Daniel's heart was heavy as he followed her because he knew what she was alluding to. Five years ago he had told her that he'd loved her, but he'd also told her that his career had meant more to him than she would ever do. No wonder she was so reluctant to believe him.

Jim Haynes was in the intensive care unit where his heart and other bodily functions were being closely monitored. He was awake and looked remarkably chirpy for someone who had undergone major surgery in the past twenty-four hours. He smiled with genuine pleasure when he saw Daniel. 'Ah, good to see you, Daniel. At least I know you won't fuss over me like these two insist on doing.'

Daniel laughed. 'I shall try my very best not to fuss, I promise you.' He pulled up a chair and sat down, trying to ignore the fact that Emma was sitting next to him. He had to stop being so aware of her and treat her as he would any colleague, politely and civilly. If he could stick to that there wouldn't be a problem.

'Good.' Jim frowned. 'So how is everything at the surgery? Emma insists that it's all going swimmingly but I doubt if she'd tell me even if it weren't. The main thing is, are you coping?'

'Yes, we are.' Daniel leant forward, feeling heat flash along his veins when his arm brushed against Emma's. Even though he was wearing a jacket he could feel the contact in every cell. He cleared his throat, keeping his gaze centred on the other man so that it wouldn't wander in her direction. It would be silly to check if she had felt that same flicker of awareness run through her.

He gave Jim a complete rundown about what had been happening. He sensed that Emma wasn't happy about him going into so much detail but he guessed that it would worry Jim more if he tried to gloss over how busy it had been. He realised he was right when he saw the frown disappear from the older man's face after he finished.

'Excellent. It's good to know the practice is in such safe hands,' Jim declared. 'Now I can let Margaret whisk me away to the cottage to recuperate without having to worry about what's going on here.'

'How did you know that I was planning on taking you to the cottage?' Margaret demanded. 'I've never even mentioned it!'

'After forty years of marriage, my dear, I can read you like an open book,' Jim told her, winking at them.

Everyone laughed at that and then Daniel stood up. 'I don't want to tire you out so I won't stay any longer. Take care of yourself, Jim, and do what your doctor orders.'

'Oh, I shall.' Jim raised his eyes to the heavens. 'I don't have a choice with this pair standing guard over me!'

Daniel was still laughing as he left ICU. He made his way along the corridor, pausing when he heard Emma calling him. He waited for her to catch him up, wondering what misdemeanour he was guilty of this time. He was already steeling himself for another tongue-lashing when she came to a halt.

'I just wanted to say that you were right. Uncle Jim did need to hear it from you that everything was all right at the surgery.'

'Oh…right…thank you.'

Daniel was so shocked that he couldn't think of anything else to say. She gave him a tight little smile then turned and hurried away. He carried on walking, only realising that he must have walked straight past the lifts when he came to the end of the corridor and could go no further. He turned around and went back the way he'd come, thinking about what Emma had said. Maybe he was reading too much into it but it was good to know that she thought he'd done something right for a change.

He groaned as he punched the button to summon the lift. How pathetic was that? A few words of praise from Emma and all of a sudden the world seemed like a much brighter place!

Emma was home well in time for evening surgery. Her aunt had returned with her but only to pack a bag. Margaret Haynes had decided to stay at a friend's house close to the hospital to save her having to make the journey back and forth. It meant that Emma and Daniel would be on their own again that night and for many more nights to come.

Emma washed her hands and then made her way round to the surgery, determined that she wasn't going to waste her time worrying about it. They were both adults and more than capable of sharing the house for the next few weeks. She was due back in Scotland in just over a month's time so it wasn't as though the situation was going to last indefinitely. Obviously, if she'd needed to take over the practice while her uncle recuperated, she would have had to arrange compassionate leave, but with Daniel here that wouldn't be necessary. He would be able to run things until Uncle Jim was well enough to return to work.

She frowned, wondering once again why Daniel had agreed to give up so much of his time to help. Although she knew that he had got on well with her uncle while he'd been doing his GP training, she hadn't realised the two men had kept in touch. Her aunt and uncle had never mentioned Daniel over the years and she certainly hadn't asked about him. She had wanted to expunge the whole unhappy episode from her life rather than dwell on it. It made her feel uneasy all of a sudden to wonder if Daniel had ever asked about her.

Emma quickly dismissed the thought as she pushed open the surgery door. Daniel had demonstrated his lack of interest five years ago in the most effective way possible!

'I'm afraid evening surgery doesn't start until four.'

Emma glanced up when she realised someone

was speaking to her. She smiled at the young woman behind the reception desk. 'You must be Claire.'

'That's right. How did you know...? Oh, you must be Emma!' The other woman blushed. 'I'm so sorry. Ruth told me that you'd probably be coming in tonight, but I was expecting someone *much* older.' She clapped her hand over her mouth, obviously wishing she hadn't said that, and Emma laughed.

'Thank you. I shall take that as a compliment. Believe me, some days I feel as old as Methuselah, so it's nice to know that I don't actually look it!' She glanced around the waiting room. 'Is Ruth not in tonight?' she asked, neatly changing the subject to spare Claire's blushes.

'Yes, but she might be a bit late. A filling fell out of one of her teeth and the dentist could only fit her in this afternoon as he's on holiday for the rest of the week,' Claire explained. 'She asked me if I'd hold the fort until she gets here. I hope that's all right.'

'Of course it is.' Emma smiled at her. 'If you have any problems, give me a buzz. I used to work on the reception desk when I was a student and I might be able to help.'

'Thanks. That's really kind of you.' Claire beamed at her. 'Daniel told me the same thing, to buzz him if I got stuck. It's the first time I've manned the desk on my own, so it's a relief to know that I can call on you two.'

'No problem.'

Emma drummed up a smile, although she could feel her hackles rising. Trust Daniel to try and worm his way into the receptionist's good books, she thought sourly, then realised how two-faced that sounded when it would appear she had done the same thing. However, her offer had been a genuine one, she assured herself as she made her way to the consulting room, aimed at making life simpler for all of them. Whereas Daniel's had undoubtedly been a way to curry favour.

She sat down at the desk, refusing to admit

that she was being unfair to him. Maybe she didn't have any proof, but everything Daniel did, he did for a reason. Look at the way he had pursued her five years ago. At the time, it had seemed that their feelings had arisen so spontaneously that she had never questioned if his were genuine. Even after they'd parted she had clung to the belief that he had genuinely felt something for her, although obviously not enough to put her before his precious career. It had taken a while before she had accepted that he had merely used her feelings for him to get her into his bed.

Emma bit her lip. It might have happened a long time ago, but it still hurt to know that she had been nothing more to him than a convenient and willing bedmate.

CHAPTER SIX

THE week came to an end and Saturday arrived. As Daniel made his way downstairs, he couldn't help wishing there was a morning surgery that day. At least if he was working, he could stay out of Emma's way.

He sighed as he went into the kitchen. To say that relations between him and Emma were strained was an understatement. She only spoke to him when it was absolutely necessary and even then it was hard to get more than a dozen words out of her. He had hoped that her attitude towards him might be softening after he'd been to visit her uncle, but obviously not. He wished he could think of a way to ease the situation but it was impossible when every time he tried to talk to her, she cut him dead.

He filled the kettle with water and popped some bread into the toaster, wondering for the umpteenth time how he could gain her trust. He wasn't a threat to her, yet she insisted on treating him like some kind of pariah, and it was very hard to take. He knew that he had hurt her but he'd been hurt too; it didn't seem fair that he should have to suffer when he had been trying to do what was right.

Daniel gave himself a brisk mental shake. Feeling sorry for himself wouldn't help. What he needed was something to take his mind off the situation and put him in a more positive frame of mind. It was a glorious day and a good long walk in the hills should blow away a lot of cobwebs.

He made himself a pot of coffee then sat down at the table to eat his breakfast. He had almost finished when Emma appeared and he sighed when he saw her stop as soon as she spotted him sitting at the table. Even the local axe murderer would receive a warmer welcome than him! He dropped the last piece of toast back onto his plate and stood up.

'Just give me a couple of seconds to wash my dishes and I'll get out of your way.'

'There's no need,' she said sharply. 'You're perfectly entitled to finish your breakfast.'

'Thank you.' It was impossible to keep the sarcasm out of his voice. 'However, I seem to have lost my appetite all of a sudden.'

He carried his dishes over to the sink. He knew that Emma was still standing in the doorway and felt pain stab through him. Had it reached the point now where she couldn't even bear to be in the same room as him?

The thought seemed to set light to his temper and he turned on the tap with far more force than was necessary. A jet of water hit the edge of his cup and bounced back up, soaking the front of his T-shirt. Daniel cursed under his breath as he hastily turned off the water. That was all he needed!

'Here.'

A hand suddenly appeared, offering him a towel. Daniel took it, trying to hide his surprise at such a conciliatory gesture. He mopped the front of his T-shirt then glanced round. Emma was standing beside him and for the first time in days she wasn't giving off the usual icy vibes. She looked up and his breath caught when he saw that her lips were twitching.

'That tap's always been a nuisance. I've had the odd soaking over the years,' she told him, struggling to contain her amusement.

'I doubt if you've been as wet as I am,' he replied drolly, shaking his head so that beads of water flew out of his hair.

'No, I haven't.' She gave a choked little gurgle. 'I know I shouldn't laugh, but if you'd seen the expression on your face…'

She burst out laughing and Daniel felt the cold knotty feeling that had been building up inside him for days suddenly start to unravel. He grinned at her, his hazel eyes sparkling with amusement.

'Think it's funny to see someone almost drowning, do you?'

'Yes… I mean, no. Of course not.' She bit her lip, doing her best to behave with suitable decorum.

Daniel chuckled wickedly. Turning on the tap, he scooped up a handful of water. 'I wonder how funny you'd find it if you were on the receiving end of an impromptu shower?'

'Daniel, you wouldn't!'

'Oh, wouldn't I?' He let a few drops of water dribble onto her bare arm, grinning when he heard her squeal in alarm. 'Are you sure about that?'

'Yes, I am.' She stared up at him and he could see the conviction in her eyes. 'You wouldn't be that cruel!'

'No, I wouldn't.' He opened his hand and let the water flow into the sink, feeling the knotty feeling start to build up inside him again. 'It's good to know that you don't think I'm completely rotten to the core, Emma.'

She didn't say anything to that and he didn't wait around while she thought of something either. He left the kitchen, taking the stairs two at a time as he headed for his room. Why in heaven's name had he said that, let her know how much it hurt to be treated as an outcast? It wouldn't achieve anything, definitely wouldn't improve her opinion of him. The last thing he wanted was for it to appear as though he was looking for sympathy!

He cursed roundly, stopping dead when he heard a knock on the door. Striding across the room, he flung it open, too angry with himself to care about putting up a front. 'Yes?'

'I just wanted to say that I'm sorry.'

Her voice was so low that it was a moment before Daniel realised what she had said. He frowned, unsure where this was leading. 'You're sorry?'

'Yes. About the way I…I've behaved recently.' She tipped back her head and looked him squarely in the eyes. 'I agreed to call a truce and I haven't kept to that. I apologise.'

'I know how difficult this situation is, Emma,' he said quietly, more touched than he cared to admit. 'I find it hard, too.'

'Do you?' She looked at him in surprise and he sighed.

'Yes. I can't just forget what happened five years ago. You meant a lot to me, Emma.'

'Did I?'

'Of course you did.' He frowned when he saw the uncertainty on her face. Surely she must know how he had felt, even though he had pushed her away? He had never tried to hide his feelings—how could he have done? She had meant the whole world to him and all of a sudden it seemed important she understood that.

'I cared a lot about you, Emma,' he said quickly, wishing that he didn't have to use such a milk-and-water term to describe how he'd felt. Claiming he'd cared barely touched on the way he had really felt about her but what else could he say? Admitting that he had loved her with every fibre of his being wasn't what she wanted to hear. His heart ached as he repeated it with as much conviction as he dared. 'I really and truly cared about you.'

'But not as much as you cared about your career.' She smiled and his heart filled with sadness when he saw the bleakness in her eyes. 'Don't worry, Daniel, I understand. And as I said the other day, it's probably a good thing that we parted. Oh, I won't pretend that it didn't hurt at the time because it did. A lot. But I'm both older and wiser, and I can see the problems it would have caused if we'd stayed together.'

'You would have regretted giving up your dreams of becoming a surgeon?' he said flatly.

'Yes. I love my job and I'm good at it, too.' She gave a little shrug. 'It was the right decision for both of us.'

'I'm glad you think so,' he said roughly. Maybe he should have been relieved to hear her say that, but all he felt was a terrible emptiness. He couldn't help wishing that he had been brave enough—or foolish enough—to take a chance and see what would happen, and it shocked him to find himself entertaining such a crazy idea. It was an effort to concentrate when she continued.

'I do. I have a job I love, good friends and a nice home. I have everything I want, in fact.'

'How about love and marriage?' he asked, then could have bitten off his tongue for asking such a personal question. Emma's love life had nothing to do with him.

'Not on my agenda at the present time. It's hard enough for a woman to establish herself in surgery without adding a husband and a family to the equation, although I haven't ruled them out completely.' She shrugged. 'If they happen at some point down the line, that's fine, but if not then I can live with it. How about you? Is there anyone special in your life?'

'No. My job seems to take up most of my time, too,' he said, not willing to admit that he had never considered the idea of marriage after they had parted.

'Still determined to set up in private practice one day?' She smiled but he could tell from her tone what she thought of the idea.

'Maybe.' He shrugged, unable to add to his guilt by deliberately misleading her again. 'Who knows what could happen in the future?'

'Who, indeed? But I'm sure you'll do everything in your power to achieve your ambitions, Daniel, won't you?'

Daniel's heart sank when he heard the suspicion in her voice. It seemed that their brief moment of harmony was over and they were back to where they had started, with Emma mistrusting his motives. Suddenly, he couldn't bear it any longer. He had to set matters straight and to hell with the consequences. 'Look, Emma, you're completely—'

He never had a chance to finish because at that moment the phone rang. Emma excused herself and went to answer it. Daniel guessed from what she said that it was her aunt calling so went back into his room. He found himself a sweater and a waterproof jacket because the weather was very changeable at this time of the year. Emma was still on the phone when he headed to the stairs; she gave him a curt little nod as he passed her then turned away, concentrating on what her aunt was saying.

Daniel left the house and walked into the town centre; there was a footpath beside the church that led up into the hills. He set off at a brisk pace, hoping the fresh air and exercise would soothe him, but it was hard to enjoy the peace and quiet when his mind was in turmoil. He hated to think that Emma was so suspicious of him but what could he do? He had forfeited her trust when he had told her that his career had meant more to him than she had done, and it was doubtful if he could win it back. Although it hurt like hell, he had to accept that Emma would never trust him again.

Emma found it hard to settle after she'd spoken

to her aunt. Aunt Margaret had told her that two of her uncle's friends were planning on visiting him that afternoon. As the number of visitors to the IC unit was strictly limited, Emma had immediately offered to wait until the following day. Now she had a free day ahead of her and suddenly found herself wondering what to do. Although there were jobs that needed doing in the house, she felt too restless to spend the day indoors. Maybe a walk would help to work off some of her excess energy.

She fetched her jacket and found an old pair of walking boots in the hall cupboard. Although she wasn't planning on going too far, she found herself taking all the usual precautions that her aunt and uncle had drummed into her over the years. The weather in the Dales could be very changeable and it was better to be prepared rather than come unstuck.

She made some sandwiches and a flask of coffee and packed them into a small haversack. After adding a map and a compass, she checked that her mobile phone was charged. Although reception was patchy in the Dales, it could come in useful. As she let herself out of the back door, she could feel her spirits lifting. It had been ages since she'd been for a good long tramp across the hills and she was suddenly looking forward to it.

The air was cool as she set off across the stile that led to the lower slopes of the hills. There were dozens of footpaths criss-crossing the area, but Emma didn't hesitate. She'd done this walk many times before and remembered the route even though it had been at least five years since she'd last been along it. She and Daniel had come this way one Sunday morning and had had a picnic at the top of the hill. And after they had finished eating they had made love, right there in the open with only the blue sky above them.

Emma blinked when she realised that she couldn't see properly. Running her hand over her eyes, she wiped away tears. She wasn't going to cry, certainly wasn't going to waste the day by thinking about the past. It was the present that mattered, nothing else. As she'd told Daniel, she liked her life the way it was and was glad that she hadn't given up her dreams for him.

She walked for almost two hours then decided to stop for a break when she reached Pilgrim's Point, a local beauty spot. Finding a sheltered area in the lea of the huge rock that marked the spot, she unzipped her jacket and laid it on the ground then sat down. Uncapping the flask, she poured herself a cup of coffee, sighing appreciatively as she inhaled the fragrant aroma. Without the usual traffic fumes to clog up her nose, everything seemed to smell so much better.

She had almost finished the coffee when she heard someone coming along the path close to where she was sitting. It was a popular route with walkers and she wasn't surprised that someone else had decided to take advantage of the weather. Glancing round, she caught a glimpse of a figure heading towards her before he disappeared into a dip in the land, but it was enough for her to recognise him. What on earth was Daniel doing here? Surely he hadn't followed her, had he? Emma's temper was already creeping up the scale when Daniel reappeared. He stopped dead and she saw the surprise on his face when he spotted her.

'Emma! What on earth are you doing here? I thought you were going to visit your uncle this afternoon?'

'Some friends of Uncle Jim's are visiting him so I decided to go for a walk instead,' she replied curtly. Although it was obvious from his reaction that he hadn't followed her, she still felt annoyed. She had been hoping for a few Daniel-free hours and it was irritating to have him turn up like this. She glowered at him. 'I was hoping to enjoy a bit of peace and quiet on my own.'

'Don't let me stop you,' he said calmly, but she saw the hurt in his eyes and immediately felt awful about being so rude. Maybe there wasn't any love lost between them nowadays but that was no excuse for the way she was behaving.

'You're not.' She gave a little shrug, unable to bring herself to actually apologise. 'I just stopped for a drink.'

Daniel sniffed the air. 'Ah, so that explains it. I thought I could smell coffee as I was coming along the path but decided I was hallucinating.' He smiled at her and her heart lifted when she saw the warmth in his eyes. 'I don't think any of the coffee-house chains has set up an outlet in the hills yet, have they?'

'Not so far as I know. It must be an oversight on their behalf,' Emma said, chuckling.

'Oh, I'm sure they'll realise that they're missing a trick,' he assured her. 'Give it a few more months and I expect you'll be able to buy your double cappuccino with hazelnut syrup on the slopes of Mount Everest!'

Emma laughed out loud. 'It wouldn't surprise me. It never fails to amaze me just how many coffee shops there are. Every town and city seems to be awash with them.'

'I have a theory about that,' Daniel said gravely.

He bent towards her and lowered his voice. 'I think they're a front for alien invaders. I mean, think about it. All those hissing and gurgling machines can't just be making cups of coffee, can they? They're probably powering up the spaceships that are hidden in the basements.'

It was so ridiculous that Emma couldn't stop laughing. She clutched her aching sides. 'Don't! I feel sick from laughing so much.'

'Sorry.' Daniel didn't sound the least bit repentant. He grinned down at her. 'I won't tell you my theory about burger bars, then.'

'Oh, please, don't! I don't think I can take any more.' Emma wiped her streaming eyes and smiled up at him, feeling her breath catch when her gaze met his. Why was Daniel looking at her that way? she wondered dizzily. He didn't love her; he never had loved her. And yet there was something in his eyes that made her heart start to race…

'Looks like the weather is about to change.'

He turned to stare across the hills and the

moment passed. Emma shuddered as she looked at the black clouds that were amassing on the horizon. Had she imagined it or had Daniel really been looking at her as though she meant the whole world to him?

She took a shaky breath when she realised how ridiculous that idea was. Daniel might care about her but only in the sort of impersonal way he would care about any woman he'd had a relationship with. She would be a fool to imagine it was anything more than that.

Emma stood up abruptly and shrugged on her jacket. Although the sun was still shining, she felt chilled to the bone and knew that it had little to do with the impending storm. Picking up the flask, she offered it to him. 'There's some coffee left if you want it.'

'Thanks.' He took the flask from her with a smile that held nothing more than gratitude. Unscrewing the lid, he filled the cup and offered it to her first. 'Do you want some more?'

'No, thank you. I've had more than enough.'

Emma could hear the edge in her voice and hated it because of what it represented. She wanted to remain indifferent to Daniel, to not allow him to affect her in any way, but it was proving impossible to achieve that. It worried her that she was so responsive to his every mood. If she was over him then she shouldn't care how he felt about anything. Including her. The thought was too much to deal with on top of everything else.

'I think I'll head back,' she informed him coolly. Bending down, she picked up the haversack and went to swing it over her shoulder, stopping abruptly when he put out his hand.

'I know this is really cheeky but those aren't sandwiches, are they?' He pointed to the package sticking out of her bag and Emma nodded.

'Yes, I thought I might have my lunch while I was out.'

'But you've changed your mind?' he suggested.

Emma could tell that he suspected he was the reason for her change of plans and shrugged.

The last thing she wanted was for Daniel to think that he could exert any sort of influence over her. 'I'd prefer to get home before the rain starts.'

'Of course. But if those sandwiches are going spare, I wouldn't mind them. I'm afraid I'm not as well prepared as you are.'

He gave her a tight little smile and Emma knew immediately that he hadn't believed her excuse. She handed him the sandwiches, refusing to dwell on the thought. Let him think what he liked—she didn't care!

'Thanks. I'll see you later, I expect.' He sat down in the spot she'd recently vacated and opened the package. Emma watched as he selected a thick ham and cheese sandwich and bit into it with relish. If he was at all disturbed about ruining her plans for the day, it certainly didn't show, she thought bitterly.

'Actually, I'm going out this evening,' she said abruptly. Although she hadn't planned on going out, the thought of spending the evening with him was suddenly more than she could bear, and she hurried on. 'I don't know when I'll be back, so I'll see you tomorrow.'

'Right. Have fun.'

Whether or not he believed her was open to question and Emma didn't waste any time worrying about it. She made her way back along the paths until she reached the stile. It had started to rain now, a fine drizzle that obscured the view of the hills. As she stepped down from the stile, she couldn't help wondering if Daniel would be all right. Although he had enjoyed walking in the area when he'd done his training here, it was easy to get lost. Maybe she should have made sure that he got back safely?

She took a deep breath. Daniel had made it clear five years ago that she had no rights where he was concerned. He wouldn't thank her for worrying about him now!

CHAPTER SEVEN

DANIEL finished the sandwiches and wadded the cling film into a ball. Tucking it into his pocket, he drained the last dregs of coffee from the cup. The clouds were fairly scurrying across the sky now and he guessed it wouldn't be long before the rain started. Maybe he should follow Emma's example and head back?

He sighed as he set off along the path. Once again he'd thought he was making headway with her and once again he'd been mistaken. It was a case of one step forward and two back, and it was difficult to explain how frustrated he felt. Maybe it was foolish to hope that she would accept him as a friend after what had happened in the past, but he couldn't bear to think that she would continue to think so badly of him.

Daniel's heart was heavy as he climbed out of the dip. The path skirted an area of loose shale and he picked his way around it, wary of slipping. The first drops of rain started to fall as he cleared the area and he picked up speed, hoping to avoid getting soaked. Although it would have been quicker if he'd taken the path Emma had used, he wasn't sure if he could remember the way. The last thing he needed to round off the day was to get himself lost!

He must have gone about a mile or so when all of a sudden he heard someone shouting. He stopped and looked around but it was difficult to see now that the rain was falling in earnest. Cupping his hands around his mouth, he shouted as loudly as he could, 'Hello! Where are you?'

'Over here,' the reply came back immediately.

Daniel turned towards the direction from where the sound seemed to be coming and frowned when he caught a glimpse of a figure frantically waving to him. What on earth was going on?

He hurriedly changed course, his heart sinking as he got closer and discovered there were actually two people, both teenage boys, and one of them was injured. 'What happened?' he demanded, crouching down beside the injured boy.

'We were just messing about, having a sword fight with a couple of sticks, when Jack slipped. I thought he was kidding at first when he didn't get up, but then I saw all the blood...' The boy gulped, obviously too shaken by what had happened to continue.

'I see.' Daniel didn't press him for any more details as he carefully eased the boy's blood-soaked T-shirt aside so he could examine the puncture wound in his chest. Although it wasn't very large, it was obviously deep and had bled copiously. He could hear the boy struggling to breathe and placed his hand over the wound. Even if the lung itself wasn't damaged, this type of injury—where air was being drawn directly into the chest cavity—could cause it to deflate

'How long ago did it happen?' he asked, glancing up.

'I'm not sure. Half an hour, maybe longer—I seem to have been shouting for ages.' The boy wiped his eyes with the back of his hand. 'I didn't know what to do. I tried to get Jack to stand up but he couldn't, so I thought about going for help. But even if I'd managed to find someone, I wasn't sure if I'd be able to find my way back here.'

'You don't have a mobile with you?' Daniel queried, dragging over a haversack and using it to support the boy's head and shoulders. He inclined the teenager's body towards the injured side so that the sound lung was uppermost then dug in his pocket and took out a clean handkerchief plus the piece of crumpled cling film. Sealing the wound to stop any more air entering the chest cavity would help the boy to breathe more easily.

'Yes, but there's no signal out here. I've tried it dozens of times but my phone just won't work!'

'Typical.' Daniel sighed as he placed the handkerchief over the hole in the boy's chest. 'Can you hold that there while I unravel this piece of cling film?' he instructed. Once he had smoothed out the plastic wrapping, he placed it over the handkerchief, pressing it tightly against the boy's damp skin. He was pleased to hear that the teenager's breathing sounded a little less laboured after he'd finished.

Standing up, he stripped off his jacket and laid it over the boy. Hypothermia was a very real concern in a situation like this and he needed to do whatever he could to avoid it. Once he was sure the boy was protected from the rain, he turned to his friend again. 'What's your name, son?'

'Ryan.'

'OK, Ryan. I'm Dr Kennedy. I work at the surgery in Avondale—do you know it?'

Ryan shook his head. 'No.'

'So can I take it that you don't live round here?'

'No. We're on a school trip. We're staying at the outward bound centre near Malham.'

'I see. So is there anyone who's likely to be looking for you right now? Your teachers, for instance?

'No. They don't know we're out here,' Ryan mumbled, looking sheepish.

'What do you mean, they don't know you're out here?'

Ryan shrugged. 'Most of the teachers have gone to Settle with the rest of the group. They're going on a train ride. Jack and I weren't allowed to go because we smuggled some beer into our dormitory last night. A couple of the boys were sick and things got a bit messy, so we had to stay behind to clean up as a punishment.'

'Surely you weren't left on your own?'

'No, one of the teachers stayed with us, but he had to go to the office to deal with a query.' Ryan looked even more uncomfortable. 'Jack and I decided to sneak out while he was gone and that's how we ended up here.'

'And found yourself in an even bigger mess from the look of it,' Daniel declared, sighing. He quickly considered their options but it was obvious what needed to be done. 'We can assume you'll be missed at some point but it could take a while before the alarm is raised and even longer before they send someone out to look for you. Quite frankly, we can't afford to wait around too long so here's what we're going to do. I'm going to stay here with Jack while you go for help. It's better if I stay with him in case anything happens.'

'But what if I can't find my way?' the boy exclaimed.

'You'll be fine,' Daniel assured him, hoping he wasn't being overly confident. 'I'll take you back to the main path and show you which way to go. So long as you stay on the path and don't wander off it, you'll be perfectly all right. It brings you out into the centre of Avondale and once you're there, just ask anyone you meet to help you.'

'But how about finding my way back here?'

Ryan asked anxiously. He glanced around and shuddered. 'All this countryside looks the same to me.'

'Have you got a watch?' Daniel unfastened his own watch when the boy shook his head and handed it to him. 'Put that on and use it to time how long it takes you to reach the town. That should give the search and rescue team a rough idea of where we are. You can also tell them that we're about a mile or so from a large rock and that Dr Roberts at the surgery can probably help to pinpoint our location if they ask her. Think you can remember all that?'

'I think so.' Ryan took a deep breath. 'Do you want me to go now?'

'Yes. Oh, and also tell them that we'll need an ambulance on standby and that they should inform the hospital to be prepared for a serious chest trauma. OK?' He smiled when Ryan nodded. 'Good. Let's get going, then. The sooner we get your friend to hospital, the better.'

Daniel led the boy back to the path and pointed

him in the right direction, repeating his instruction to stay on the path and not wander off it. He frowned as he watched him set off, hoping he was doing the right thing by sending him for help, but what choice did he have? He couldn't go because he needed to stay with Jack.

He sighed as he made his way back to the injured boy. What was that saying about the road to hell being paved with good intentions? Although his intentions may have been good five years ago, look how badly things had turned out then. Hopefully, there would be a happier outcome this time.

Emma decided to go to the cinema in the end. Although it was a bit of trek to the nearest town that boasted a cinema, it would be worth it. If she set off early, she could do some shopping first and then watch the film. She may as well go for a meal afterwards too. Then she could keep out of Daniel's way for the rest of the day.

She groaned as she stepped into the shower.

She couldn't continue avoiding him. Whether she liked the idea or not, she and Daniel were going to have to get along for the next few weeks both in and out of the surgery. Maybe there was a lot of history between them but the key word in that statement was *history.* Their relationship was in the past and it shouldn't have any bearing on what happened at the present time. She'd been out with other men in the past few years and remained on good terms with them too. If she could get it into her head that Daniel was just someone she had once dated, she could put it behind her.

She got dressed and went downstairs. She was just unhooking her jacket off the hall peg when she heard a car pull up outside and frowned. She wasn't expecting visitors and had no idea who it could be. Opening the door, she blinked in surprise when she saw one of the local search and rescue vehicles parked outside. Although her uncle had been a member of the team for many years, he had been forced to retire when his health had started to deteriorate. She couldn't imagine what they were doing here and waited expectantly as Mike Harding, the team leader, hurried towards her.

'Looks as though we've arrived in the nick of time,' Mike observed jovially. A pleasant man in his forties who ran the local pub with his wife, April, he'd been leading the local team for the past ten years. 'I take it that you were on your way out?'

'I was,' Emma agreed. 'I was just about to head off to the cinema, in fact. Why? Is there a problem?'

'Seems like it.' Mike pointed towards a boy sitting in the front passenger seat. 'According to that young fellow, his friend is out in the Dales somewhere, injured, and Dr Kennedy is with him.'

'Daniel!' Emma exclaimed. 'Are you sure?'

'As sure as I can be. The lad came stumbling into the pub about ten minutes ago and told us that his friend was hurt and that there was a man with him who said he was a doctor.' Mike shrugged. 'April asked him to describe him and she said that it sounded very much like Dr Kennedy.'

'She's probably right,' Emma said slowly. 'Daniel did go for a walk this morning. In fact, I met him while I was out.'

'And where was that?' Mike said quickly. 'Apparently, Dr Kennedy told the lad to tell us that he was about a mile from a large rock and that you'd know where it was.'

'He must mean Pilgrim's Point,' Emma told him. 'I was sitting there when I saw Daniel.'

'Great!' Mike beamed at her. 'It doesn't half help when folk are able to narrow down the search area. I'll get on the radio and let the others know where we're heading.'

Emma followed him back to the car, waiting quietly as he put through a call to the rest of the team. 'Do we know how badly injured the other boy is?' she asked as soon as he finished.

'Chest injury, apparently. Your Dr Kennedy

told the lad to tell us to have an ambulance on standby and to inform the hospital to prepare for a serious chest trauma.'

Emma felt her face heat. He wasn't *her* Dr Kennedy; he never had been hers in any way, shape or form. It was on the tip of her tongue to point that out until she realised how silly it was to make a fuss. She was supposed to be trying to think of Daniel as just another ex-boyfriend!

'It might be best to have the air ambulance on standby,' she suggested, confining her thoughts to the matter at hand.

'We've already done that,' Mike informed her. 'Air Ambulance Control has logged the request, although they can't guarantee another call won't come in in the meantime.'

'Of course not,' Emma agreed, shivering as she glanced towards the hills. The rain was much heavier now, a heavy blanket of clouds overhead stealing the light from the day. Although it was barely the middle of the afternoon, it looked more like evening. She knew that the longer

Daniel and the boy were missing, the greater the risk of them not being found before night fell. The thought spurred her to a swift decision.

'I'm coming with you.' She held up her hand when Mike started to protest that it wasn't necessary. 'No, I want to come. I'll be able to help with the boy if nothing else. Give me two minutes to change and I'll be right with you.'

She ran back into the house, quickly exchanging her lightweight jacket for something more suitable. Her walking boots were on the mat where she'd left them and it took only seconds to slip them on. She knew the team carried basic medical supplies as a matter of course so didn't need to worry about that. Within a couple of minutes she was back at the Land Rover.

'Ready,' she told Mike as she climbed into the rear seat. She could feel her tension building as they drove into the centre of the town. The rest of the team was gathered outside the church. There were about a dozen altogether, all of them volunteers.

Emma nodded hello then stood to one side while Mike spread an Ordnance Survey sheet on the bonnet of the car. He ringed Pilgrim's Point in red then turned to the boy. Emma bit her lip when Ryan explained that it had taken him just over two hours to reach the town. It was already three o'clock, which meant it would be going dark before they got back to where Daniel was waiting and that was assuming they could pinpoint his location. Finding people lost in the Dales wasn't easy, as any member of the team would confirm.

She took a deep breath as Mike folded up the map. The thought of Daniel being at risk was more than she could bear, even though she refused to ask herself why.

Without a watch to refer to, Daniel had no idea how much time had passed since Ryan had gone for help. It seemed to be hours since the boy had left yet he knew that it was probably his mind playing tricks. As he checked Jack's pulse again, he found himself praying that help would arrive soon. The boy had lapsed into unconsciousness a while ago and there was no doubt that his condition was deteriorating. He needed to be admitted to hospital as quickly as possible if he was to have any chance of pulling through.

The thought had barely crossed his mind when the boy suddenly stopped breathing. Daniel quickly rolled him onto his back and checked his airway. Once he was sure it was clear, he pinched Jack's nostrils closed and breathed into his mouth, sharply, four times to inflate his lungs. He then checked his pulse and was relieved to find that his heart was still beating. He breathed into his mouth again and continued doing so for several more minutes until Jack started breathing for himself again.

After placing the boy in the recovery position, Daniel stood up, groaning as he stretched his aching limbs. He was soaking wet, thanks to the rain, and freezing cold too. He jumped up and down to try to generate some warmth in his body, flapping his arms as well for good measure. It helped a bit but he knew that the effects wouldn't last. Night was drawing in and the temperature would drop even lower then. What wouldn't he give to be sitting in front of a roaring fire with Emma curled up beside him…?

He blanked out that thought. He was feeling miserable enough without making himself feel even worse because the chances of Emma ever curling up beside him were nil!

Although Emma must have walked along the route dozens of times before, she had never attempted it in such appalling weather. The rain was beating down now, turning the path into a sea of mud in places, so that it was difficult to keep her footing. It didn't help either that some of the streams had burst their banks, forcing them to wade ankle deep through icy-cold water. It was only the thought of Daniel and the injured boy waiting for them that kept her going. They had to find them.

'OK, let's stop for a moment while we get our bearings.' Mike called the group to a halt, waiting until they had formed a circle before he continued. 'By my reckoning, we should be fairly close to where young Ryan here said he left his friend so we'll split up into groups and see if we can find him and the doc.'

Everyone nodded. Within a very short time they had formed four groups. Mike turned to Emma. 'You and the lad can come with me. They can't be far from here so let's hope we can find them pretty soon.'

He didn't add anything else as he started walking again but he didn't need to. Emma knew that once it got dark, the chances of them finding the pair were very slim. She and Ryan followed the others along the track, scouring the land to right and left in the hope of spotting them. They came to a slight rise in the ground and Ryan suddenly stopped.

'I remember this bit!' he exclaimed excitedly.

'How far is it from where you left your friend?' Mike demanded.

'Not very far, I think…ten, twenty metres, something like that,' the boy told him.

'Right then, let's start shouting and see if they can hear us.' Mike cupped his hands round his mouth. 'Hello! Can you hear us? Are you out there, Doc?'

Emma held her breath. Ryan seemed so certain that surely he couldn't have been mistaken? Mike shouted again but there was still no reply and her heart sank. They carried on for another few minutes and then Mike stopped and repeated the process. When a voice suddenly shouted back she didn't know whether to laugh or cry because she felt so overwhelmed with emotion. It was all she could do to stumble after the others as they hurried towards where the sound had come from.

'Am I glad to see you,' Daniel began, standing up. He suddenly caught sight of her and Emma saw the shock on his face. It was blatantly obvious that he hadn't expected to see her and all of a sudden she felt uncomfortable about her reasons for being there.

Crossing the narrow strip of ground that separated them, she crouched down beside the injured boy, busying herself with doing his obs while Daniel conferred with Mike. Although she could hear what was being said, it seemed to be happening at one step removed from her. It was only when Daniel crouched down beside her that everything snapped back into focus.

'I'll set up a drip,' she said crisply, starting to rise, but he caught her hand and stopped her.

'I didn't expect you to come, Emma.'

'No?' She gave a little shrug, hoping it would convince him that her reasons had had little to do with him. 'I thought you might need help, that's all. With the boy.'

'That was good of you. Thank you.'

His voice was low but she could hear the note it held and her heart reacted immediately to it. She stood up abruptly and hurried over to where

Mike had left the bag of medical supplies. Saline, antiseptic wipes, cannula… She mentally listed all the things she needed because it was safer to concentrate on them than on anything else, far safer than letting herself think about the way Daniel had looked at her just now.

She took a deep breath, held it until she felt dizzy, then let it out as slowly as she could, but the thought didn't flow away with it. It seemed to be stuck in her head, neon bright and incredibly scary: Daniel had been pleased to see her, surprised but pleased. What did it mean?

CHAPTER EIGHT

DANIEL could feel his heart thumping as he helped Emma set up the drip. It had been a shock to see her and there was no point denying it. Had she come purely to offer her services as a doctor, or because she had been worried about him?

His heart beat all the harder at that beguiling thought and he gritted his teeth. He was doing it again, letting himself hope for the impossible, and it was stupid to behave this way. Emma's reasons for being here had nothing to do with him and everything to do with their patient!

He stood up abruptly and turned to Mike. 'That's about all we can do for him. The sooner we get him to hospital, the better his chances will be.'

'The air ambulance is on its way,' Mike informed him. 'The problem is that it can't land out here in the dark—it's way too dangerous. We're going to have to carry the lad to the nearest stretch of road and have him picked up from there.'

'How long's that going to take?' Daniel demanded, his heart sinking at the thought of there being a further lengthy delay.

'Fifteen minutes max,' Mike assured him.

'But it takes a lot longer than that to get back to town,' Daniel protested.

'It does, but I expect the team will use a different route to get him to the road,' Emma said quietly beside him.

Daniel spun round, feeling his senses reel when he realised how close she was. Normally, she kept her distance, both physically and mentally, but she was standing so close to him now that he could feel the warmth of her skin. It was hard to concentrate when every cell in his body was so acutely aware of her.

'Do you mean to say that I could have got help

here sooner if I hadn't sent Ryan into the town?' he demanded, the force of his reaction making him sound—and *feel*—distinctly tetchy.

'I doubt it. The nearest road to here is fairly isolated. There's very little traffic uses it, especially at this time of the year, so the chances of Ryan being able to flag down a car were pretty remote. You did the best thing by sending him back to town to get help,' she replied calmly, although Daniel couldn't help noticing that she avoided meeting his eyes.

Was she equally aware of him as he was of her? he wondered, then had to swallow his groan when his heart set off again, pounding away as though possessed. When Mike came over with a foil blanket for him to wrap around himself, he barely managed to nod his thanks. Forget about feeling cold and wet—it would be a miracle if he didn't have a heart attack at this rate!

It took them just under the allotted time to stretcher the injured boy to the pick-up point. The police were already there and had set up a landing site for the helicopter in a nearby field. It arrived a couple of minutes later and Daniel handed over his patient, briefly explaining to the crew what had happened and what he had done. Five minutes later, it was on its way again. The police had also contacted the outward-bound centre where the two boys were staying and one of the teachers had come to collect Ryan. From the glum expression on the teenager's face as he got into the car, Daniel guessed that he wasn't expecting much of a welcome when he got back.

'That's it, folks. Let's just hope the lad will be all right, eh?'

Mike voiced everyone's opinion as they headed over to the vehicles. A couple of the reserve team had driven over to collect them and Daniel had to admit that it was a relief not to have to walk all the way back to town. Now that the adrenalin rush was dying down, he felt too cold and stiff to welcome the thought of a long walk home.

He slid into the back of one of the vehicles, moving over when Emma got in beside him.

Another member of the team climbed in beside her so it was a bit of a squash. Daniel held himself rigid as they set off but it was impossible to avoid touching her as they swung around the bends.

'Sorry,' he murmured when once again he found himself cannoning into her.

'That's OK.'

She gave him a tight little smile then stared straight ahead, making it clear that she wasn't keen to start a conversation. He wasn't either, mainly because he didn't want anything he said to be misconstrued. He sighed wearily. When had life become so complicated that he had to watch every word he said?

Emma couldn't wait to get home. Sitting beside Daniel was sheer torture. Every time they rounded a bend, his shoulder brushed hers or his thigh pressed against her thigh and she didn't appreciate the feelings it aroused inside her. It was a relief when the car drew up outside the house.

Daniel got out and offered her his hand but she pretended not to see it. Sliding across the seat, she got out and thanked the driver. The car drove away with a toot of its horn, its taillights rapidly disappearing into the darkness. Emma headed towards the front door, feeling her tension mounting when she heard Daniel's footsteps crunching on the gravel behind her. All of a sudden she was achingly aware of the fact that there were just the two of them. She would have given anything to open the door and find Aunt Margaret at home but it wasn't going to happen so she had to make the best of things. Unlocking the front door, she summoned a smile.

'I'll put the kettle on while you get out of those wet clothes. Do you prefer tea or coffee?'

'Coffee, please.' Daniel grimaced as he stepped into the hall. 'I'm soaking. I'd better take my clothes off here rather than drip water all through the house.'

He shed the foil blanket then dragged his sodden sweater over his head. Emma just caught a glimpse of a broad, muscled chest before she hastily turned away.

'I'll get the coffee on,' she murmured, hurrying along the hall as though the hounds of hell were snapping at her heels. She filled the kettle then took off her wet coat and carried it through to the back porch so it could drip. When she chanced a wary glance along the hall there was no sign of Daniel, just a heap of sodden clothing lying neatly on the mat.

She ran upstairs to her room and changed into dry jeans then went back down and gathered up Daniel's clothing to take it through to the kitchen, putting his sweater and jeans straight into the washer. His boots were soaked so she stuffed them with newspaper and left them in the corner to dry. By the time she'd done all that, he reappeared, shaking his head as he came into the kitchen.

'You shouldn't have cleared up after me, Emma. I'd have done it myself.'

'It wasn't a problem,' she said lightly, not wanting him to attach any significance to her actions. She had done it purely because she liked order in her life, not because she'd wanted to help him, she assured herself. She headed towards the kettle then stopped when he waved her aside.

'*I'll* make the coffee. It's the least I can do.'

Emma opened her mouth then hurriedly shut it again. Arguing about who should make the coffee would be extremely childish. Walking over to the cupboard, she lifted out the biscuit tin and set it on the table. When Daniel brought over the tray, he looked hopefully at her.

'I hope there's some chocolate biscuits in there. There's nothing like comfort food when you're feeling cold and miserable.'

'There should be.' Emma took the lid off the tin and nodded. 'You're in luck. There's a new packet of chocolate digestives—your favourites.'

'So you remember which biscuits I like?' His

tone was even but she felt the blood rush up her face when she realised how revealing that had been. If she had erased him from her life then why on earth would she remember his taste in food?

'Yes,' she said firmly, knowing there was no point lying. She looked him straight in the eyes. 'I'm hardly likely to forget, bearing in mind the amount of biscuits you consumed when you worked here.'

'Hmm, I suppose not.' He grinned. 'I *could* claim that I'm a reformed character and only eat them in exceptional circumstances but that would be cutting off my nose to spite my face.' He helped himself to a biscuit. 'All I can say is that it's my only vice, or the only one I'm willing to admit to!'

He chuckled as he bit into the biscuit and Emma felt a little flurry of heat run through her veins. She had forgotten how endearing he could be when he was poking fun at himself.

The thought troubled her and she picked up

the pot, quickly pouring coffee into two mugs. She didn't want to think about Daniel's good points, certainly didn't want to remember the reasons why she had fallen in love with him. She needed to focus on the way he had treated her. She had been willing to give up her dreams for him but it hadn't been enough. His career had meant far more to him than what she could have given him.

Pain lanced her heart and she took a gulp of her coffee then coughed when the hot liquid shot down the wrong way. Putting the mug down on the table, she tried to catch her breath but it felt as though her lungs had gone into spasm.

'Are you all right?' Daniel leant forward and looked at her in concern. 'Emma?'

Emma tried to answer but there was no way that she could force out even a single word and she saw him leap to his feet. Moving swiftly behind her chair he slapped her on the back and with relief she felt the constriction loosen. Sucking in a deep breath, she finally managed to speak.

'I'm all right now.'

'Sure?' He went over to the sink when she nodded and filled a glass with cold water and gave it to her. 'Take a couple of sips of this.'

Emma obediently sipped the water then set the glass on the table, feeling embarrassed about having caused such a fuss. 'Some of the coffee must have gone down the wrong way.'

'Easily done,' he said lightly, sitting down again. He slid the biscuit tin across the table. 'Aren't you going to have one?'

'I'm not sure if I should risk it after what just happened,' she said wryly.

Daniel laughed. 'Go on—live dangerously. Anyway, I'm a dab hand at the Heimlich manoeuvre if the need arises.'

Emma grimaced as she selected a biscuit. 'Let's hope it doesn't come to that.'

'Fingers crossed,' he said, suiting his actions to his words.

Emma chuckled as she bit into her biscuit. Daniel had a real gift when it came to putting people at ease. Some of the doctors she had worked with seemed to enjoy feeling superior, but Daniel wasn't like that. He cared too much about other people to want them to feel uncomfortable around him.

The thought surprised her because it didn't gel with the image she had held of him for the past few years. If Daniel was the single-minded, ambitious man she had believed him to be, surely he wouldn't care about anyone else's feelings?

'Penny for them.'

Emma looked up when he spoke, feeling her heart lurch when she saw the way he was watching her so intently. Why did she have the feeling that he really wanted to know what was troubling her? She had no idea but it was that thought which made her reply without pausing to consider the wisdom of what she was doing. 'I was just thinking what a contradiction you are.'

'Really?' His brows rose as he picked up his

mug of coffee. He took a sip of the hot liquid then placed the mug carefully back on the table. 'In what way?'

'Well, you've never made any bones about the fact that you're very ambitious, have you, Daniel? And yet in some respects you don't fit that bill.' She shrugged when he looked quizzically at her. 'You genuinely seem to care about people and it's rare that the two go hand in hand.'

'Of course I care. I wouldn't have gone into medicine if I hadn't.'

Emma frowned when she heard the edge in his voice, wondering if she had touched a nerve. 'One doesn't always follow the other,' she pointed out. 'I've worked with a number of doctors who openly admitted that they decided on medicine purely because it seemed like a good career choice.'

'They're the exceptions. Or I hope they are.' He stared down at the mug he was holding. 'In my opinion you can't do this job properly unless you genuinely want to help people.'

'So how does your desire to help people equate with wanting to go into private practice? Surely you could help far more people by working for the NHS?'

'Rich people get sick too, Emma.' He glanced up and she was surprised when she saw the sadness on his face because she wasn't sure what had caused it. 'Having money doesn't protect you from all the usual ailments.'

'I know that.' She leant forward, suddenly impatient to get to the bottom of this mystery. The more she thought about it, the stranger it seemed that Daniel of all people should be so keen to follow this course. 'And I'm not suggesting that people who can afford it shouldn't have the right to choose to pay for their treatment. But setting yourself up in private practice doesn't seem like something you would want to do. I just can't understand it, if I'm honest.'

Daniel wasn't sure what to say. If he admitted that he'd never had any intention of going into private practice, he would have to tell her the truth. How would she feel if he admitted that he had deliberately misled her? Hurt, angry, upset; she was bound to feel all of those things. But would she understand that he had been trying to protect her, stop her doing something she would regret?

'What's to understand?' he said shortly, knowing it was a risk he wasn't prepared to take. 'Everyone has their aims in life, including you. What made *you* decide to become a surgeon?'

'Because I saw how surgery could improve people's lives when I did my rotations,' she said simply. 'That's why I chose it.'

'There you are, then. You chose your path and I chose mine. It's as simple as that.' He stood up abruptly, pushing back his chair so fast that the legs scraped across the tiles. 'I think I'll have an early night. Hopefully, a good night's sleep will ease some of the kinks out of my aching muscles.'

'Of course. I'll see you in the morning, I expect.'

'If I manage to drag myself out of bed.'

Daniel summoned a smile but it was a poor effort, he knew. He left the kitchen and headed upstairs to his room. Switching on the bedside lamp, he sank down on the bed, wishing with all his heart that he could have done things differently five years ago. Letting Emma go had been the hardest thing he had ever done yet he was more convinced than ever that it had been the right thing to do. Maybe they would have had a few years of happiness together, but eventually she would have regretted giving up her dreams to be with him.

He took a deep breath. No matter how hard it had been, it would have been so much worse if Emma had ended up hating him.

Emma spent a couple of hours watching television after Daniel retired to his room. The plans she'd made to go to the cinema had been put on hold because she couldn't be bothered getting ready to go out. However, by the time the old grandfather clock in the hall struck nine, she was bored stiff. She switched off the set and made her way upstairs. She reached the landing and paused to listen but there was no sound coming from Daniel's side of the house. Obviously, he was fast asleep, worn out after his exertions that day.

Emma went to her room and collected her toilet bag then made her way to the bathroom. She felt too restless to sleep and was hoping that a long, hot soak in the bath would help her relax. Turning on the taps, she added a generous dollop of bubble bath to the water then stripped off her clothes. Water had been in short supply where she had been working recently and it was a luxury to be able to fill the bath almost to the brim.

She slid into the scented bubbles with an appreciative groan and closed her eyes. Whether it was the warmth of the water or the silence, she soon drifted off to sleep only to awake with a start when the bathroom door suddenly opened.

Emma's eyes shot open as she stared at Daniel in dismay.

'What are you doing? Get out!'

'I'm sorry. I had no idea you were in here. The door wasn't locked,' he began, then stopped.

Emma saw him swallow and looked down, feeling her heart leap when she realised that all the bubbles had melted away while she'd slept. Without them to conceal her, her body was naked to his gaze and she could tell that the sight was having an effect. Water sloshed over the side of the bath as she scrambled to her feet and reached for a towel off the rail, but Daniel was ahead of her.

'Here.' He passed her a towel then turned away while she wrapped it around herself.

Emma stepped out of the bath, shaking her wet hair out of her eyes. She felt both cold and shivery, and it owed little to the fact that she'd been lying in the cooling water for too long. Daniel wanted her: she had seen it in his eyes, seen the desire that had filled them just now. The thought should have repulsed her but it didn't—just the opposite, in fact. Heat suddenly scorched along her veins when she realised with a jolt of shock that she wanted him too….

Afterwards, she was never sure what happened next, whether she made some sort of small betraying sound or it was sheer coincidence that he turned at that moment. There was a second when their eyes locked and held before he slowly reached out and touched her cheek.

'Emma.'

Her name sounded so different when he said it that way, his deep voice throbbing with hunger and need. Emma wasn't aware of moving yet all of a sudden she was standing in front of him, so close that she could feel the tremor that passed through his body. When his hand lifted to her face again, she didn't move, just stood there while his fingers grazed along her jaw, gliding so lightly over her skin that it was hard to know for sure if he was actually touching her.

'Your skin's so soft,' he whispered as his fingers came to rest a millimetre away from her mouth.

Emma knew that if she dipped her head the barest fraction she would feel them on her lips and the thought was the sweetest kind of torment. She wanted him to touch her mouth but she wasn't sure where it would lead if he did. Could she allow Daniel to touch her, caress her, *make love* to her, and not feel anything except desire? Maybe it was what she needed to finally get him out of her system. Although she had been out with other men since they had split up, she had never wanted to sleep with any of them. In the beginning she had been too wary of getting hurt to risk getting involved and, more recently, she had been so busy in work that she'd had no time for a private life—or so she had told herself. Now Emma found herself wondering if the truth was far more complicated: she had never really drawn a line under her affair with Daniel so that she could move on.

This could be the perfect opportunity to do so,

but still she hesitated. Her feelings for Daniel were so muddled up. Although sleeping with him might give her the closure she needed, it might achieve just the opposite result. What if she found that the old feelings she'd had for him, the ones she had thought were dead and buried a long time ago, were still very much alive? It was the uncertainty that scared her, the thought that she might regret whichever decision she made for the rest of her life.

CHAPTER NINE

DANIEL could feel his heart racing. It wasn't just this desire he felt to take Emma in his arms and make love to her that was causing it to happen but fear as well. For the past five years he had kept his emotions strictly under wraps. It hadn't been difficult. He had never had a proper relationship with another woman since they had split up and had never wanted one. Although he dated frequently, he steadfastly avoided commitment. Whenever he made love to a woman, it was a purely physical experience: he had remained emotionally detached. However, he knew he wouldn't be able to do that with Emma.

Fear turned his guts to ice and he froze. Emma was standing stock still as well and he sensed that she was fighting her own inner battle about what should happen. He was already preparing himself for the inevitable rejection when her head dipped just a fraction. He sucked in his breath when he felt her mouth brush his fingers. Heat surged through his veins, melting away the fear that had filled him only moments before. He wanted her so much, wanted to bury himself in her softness and sweetness while they made love. Maybe it was madness and maybe he would regret it later but right now he needed this more than he had needed anything in his life!

He drew her into his arms and it was like coming home. Her body felt so sweetly familiar as it nestled against him, each soft curve fitting so perfectly that he didn't have to think how he should hold her—he just did. He could feel her breasts pressing against his chest and closed his eyes as a wave of pure pleasure swept over him. She felt so right in his arms that the years they'd spent apart might never have happened.

'Daniel?'

Her voice was low, the uncertainty it held filling him with tenderness. Bending, her touched her mouth with his in a kiss that was meant to reassure and calm her fears. However, the moment his lips tasted hers desire took over. He pulled her to him, letting her feel the effect she was having on him, and felt her tremble. There wasn't a doubt in his mind that she was equally affected and his heart overflowed with joy. Even after everything that had happened, Emma still wanted him!

He kissed her again with a passion that immediately had her clinging to him. When her lips opened, inviting him to deepen the kiss, he groaned. He was shaking by the time he drew back but so was she. Cupping her face between his hands, he looked deep into her eyes, hoping she could see how much this meant to him.

'I want to make love to you, Emma, more than anything, but are you sure it's what you really want?'

'Yes.' Her voice was still low but there was

a conviction in it now that reassured him she knew exactly what she was doing. 'It's what I want too, Daniel.'

'Good.'

He smiled as he bent and kissed her again. When he lifted her up into his arms, she rested her head on his shoulder. He carried her back to her room and laid her down on the narrow single bed then sat down beside her. Reaching out, he tugged gently on the folds of damp towel, feeling his breath catch when they parted to reveal her body to his gaze. Her breasts were high and full, the rose-pink nipples standing erect and proud beneath his gaze. Her waist was narrow, her hips curved, her thighs smooth and firm. Every tiny inch of her was so perfect that for a moment he was overwhelmed by her beauty and couldn't move. It was only when she placed her hand on his that the spell was broken.

He lifted her hand to his mouth and pressed a kiss against her palm. 'You're beautiful, Emma,' he whispered, his voice grating with the force of his desire.

'Am I?' She smiled at him, her green eyes heavy with passion.

'Yes. More beautiful than any woman I've ever known.'

He kissed her palm again then gently placed her hand by her side while his fingers trailed across her wrist and up her arm. He paused when he came to her shoulder. Her skin was still slightly damp from her bath and he allowed himself a moment to savour its warmth and moistness under his fingertips. When his hand moved on, following the line of her collarbone, he heard her murmur and smiled. This was one journey they were both enjoying making together.

His fingers traced the delicate bones until they came to her throat where once again they lingered. Daniel could feel her pulse beating, could feel it racing, in fact, but as his was racing too it didn't seem strange. Bending, he let the tip of his tongue touch the spot where it beat so strongly and felt her shudder, and shuddered too, more affected by her response than he would have believed. In that second he realised just how different it was making love to Emma than to any other woman. Whatever she felt, he felt too; they were that much in tune.

The thought almost blew him away but there were more delights awaiting him and he wanted to savour them all. His hand glided down her throat, following the lines of her body as it skated over the swell of her breasts, the dip of her waist, the curve of her hips. He could have stopped at any one of those places, and remained there quite happily too, but he was greedy to reacquaint himself with every inch of her delectable body.

Her thighs came next, then her knees and her ankles followed by her feet. As he caressed her toes, Daniel knew that he would never feel this depth of desire for any other woman. It was only Emma he had ever wanted so totally, only Emma he had ever loved so completely.

Emma could feel the desire building inside her as Daniel continued to stroke and caress every inch of her body. He had always been a considerate lover, taking time and care to ensure that she enjoyed their love-making as much as he did. She'd had a couple of brief affairs before she had met him, but nobody had ever made her feel as loved and as cherished as Daniel did. When his hand began its upward journey, retracing the route it had taken, she closed her eyes, relishing the touch of his fingers as they glided over her skin. She knew that she had given in to temptation and that she might regret it later, but at that moment it didn't seem to matter. All she wanted right now was to feel: his hand on her thighs, on her belly, her breasts….

Desire shot through her, red-hot and urgent, when his hand was replaced by his mouth as he took her nipple between his lips and suckled her, and she gasped. She had forgotten how intensely Daniel could make her feel, how he could carry her to a peak of need and then take her even higher. No man had ever done that apart from him. No man ever would.

Pain lanced her heart at the thought but there was no time to dwell on it because his mouth had moved to her other breast. Once again there was that surge of desire that made her stomach muscles clench and her senses reel. When he raised his head, Emma was no longer capable of thinking, only feeling, and he must have realised that. His mouth skimmed up her throat and captured hers in a kiss so raw, so filled with passion that it seemed to consume her totally. She could barely breathe when he drew back but, then, neither could he. They looked at one another for a long moment and she could see the same wonderment in his eyes that she knew must be in hers.

'Emma, I…'

He stopped and shook his head, although whether it was because he couldn't find the words to describe how he felt or because he was reluctant to say them, she wasn't sure, and maybe it was for the best. Even though she had no idea what would happen later, she knew that this wasn't the start of something more. Passion was one thing but love was something completely different and she knew for certain that Daniel didn't love her.

Tears filled her eyes but she blinked them away. She refused to cry. The past was over, the future unknown; it was the here and now that mattered. When Daniel stood up and stripped off his clothes, she focused on the moment, nothing more. And when he lay down beside her and took her in his arms, she let their passion sweep her away to a place where nothing else existed except her and Daniel and the magic they were creating together.

The air was cool when Daniel awoke the following morning. The central heating hadn't switched on yet and the temperature had dropped considerably through the night. Leaning over, he carefully drew the quilt over Emma's shoulders, resisting the urge he felt to kiss her awake. They had made love several times during the night and it wouldn't be fair to wake her when she needed to sleep.

He sighed as he swung his legs out of bed and stood up. Had it been fair to make love to her in the first place? Last night he'd been carried away by his desire for her but now it was time to face up to what he had done. He had made love to Emma when he had known in his heart that it was the last thing he should have done. It made no difference that she had been as eager and as willing as he'd been; he should have had the strength to resist temptation. He would never forgive himself if he ended up hurting her through his selfishness.

Daniel's heart was heavy as he made his way to the bathroom. Switching on the shower, he let the hot water pound down on his head and shoulders. However, if he'd hoped that it would wash away some of the guilt he felt then he was disappointed. Last night shouldn't have happened and there was no excuse for his actions. All he could do now was to try and lessen the damage he may have caused.

He went to his room and dressed then made his way to the kitchen. As soon as the kettle boiled he made himself a cup of instant coffee and sat down at the table while he tried to work out how he should handle things. So much depended on how Emma felt about the situation, of course. Would she be stricken with guilt too? He hoped not. Emma wasn't to blame for the fact that he had been unable to control himself!

'Stop it, Daniel.'

The sound of her voice brought his head up. Daniel's heart gave an almighty lurch when he saw her standing in the doorway. She was wearing a thick towelling robe and he knew without having to be told that she wasn't wearing anything under it. Heat scorched along his veins and he cursed soundlessly. He couldn't afford to dwell on thoughts like that when he had to make sure that Emma didn't come to any harm.

'I don't know what you mean,' he said, his voice sounding unnaturally gruff as he tried to work out how to salvage the situation.

'Of course you do.' She came into the room and stood in front of the table. 'You're sitting there, wallowing in guilt because of what happened last night, and it's so typically arrogant of you.'

'Arrogant?' His brows shot skywards and he looked at her in surprise.

'Yes.' Resting her hands on the edge of the table she bent so that she could look straight into his eyes. 'You didn't coerce me into bed, neither did you have your *wicked way* with me. I made love with you because I wanted to. If I hadn't wanted to, it would never have happened. Is that clear?'

'Yes.' He was so stunned by her forthright approach that he couldn't think what else to say but Emma didn't seem to expect him to say anything.

'Good. The last thing I need is you thinking

that I'm holding out for a reconciliation.' She gave a sharp laugh. 'Last night was fun and I enjoyed it but that's as far as it went. It certainly wasn't the start of something more.'

'That's how I feel too,' Daniel said thickly. Even though he knew he should be relieved that she felt this way, he couldn't help feeling hurt that their love-making had meant so little to her.

'It seems we're in agreement, then.' She gave him a cool little smile and went to switch on the kettle.

Daniel finished his coffee in a couple of quick gulps and excused himself. Emma was making toast when he left the kitchen, acting as though everything was completely normal, and maybe it was for her. Maybe she'd had a string of lovers in the past few years, men she had enjoyed the odd night of passion with. She'd mentioned her boss, hadn't she? Richard something-or-other. Maybe he was one of them, although there could be a long line of past and present suitors for all he knew. Although he hated the idea, what right did he have to criticise how she lived her life? The truth was that he had forfeited any rights where Emma was concerned five years ago. She was free to do whatever she wished.

The thought was so agonising that Daniel knew he had to get out of the house before he made a fool of himself. Unhooking his coat off the peg, he let himself out of the front door. His car was parked in the drive so he got in and started the engine. When he reached the main road, he headed towards Harrogate purely because it was somewhere to aim for. He wasn't heading *to* somewhere but away from a place where it was too painful to be. The trouble was that no matter how many miles he put between himself and Emma, it didn't stop him thinking about her, definitely didn't stop him wishing that things could have been different.

Emma managed to maintain her composure until she heard Daniel's car driving away. She sank down onto a chair, feeling sick and shaken by what had happened. She had known the moment she had seen him sitting at the table that he had regretted what had happened the night before. It had been pride that had helped her deal with the situation, pride plus the fear of what might happen if he realised how much it had meant to her.

She bit her lip, overwhelmed by a sudden feeling of dread. Making love with Daniel had been everything she could have wished for but she wasn't foolish enough to think that it had meant anything special to him. Maybe he had desired her but that was all it had been. Whilst she had tried to convince herself that it would be the ideal way to draw a line under the past, she doubted if Daniel had viewed it that way. He hadn't needed to because he had got over her a long time ago. There was no way that had he been celibate for the past five years, and last night she had been just another in a long line of women willing and eager to give him pleasure.

The thought of Daniel making love to all those other women was incredibly painful, so Emma tried not to dwell on it. There were just two weeks left of her stay and after that she would return to the life she had built for herself. It had taken her a long time to get over Daniel the last time and she couldn't bear to think that she would have to go through that kind of heartache again, so she would make sure he didn't gain any kind of hold over her. And that meant there must never be a repeat of what had happened last night.

Daniel was snatching five minutes' break in the middle of what had turned out to be an extremely busy Monday morning surgery when Emma knocked on his door.

'Ruth said you didn't have a patient with you at the moment,' she explained as she came into the room.

'I was just taking a breather,' he replied, hoping he sounded calmer than he felt.

He had managed to stay out of her way for the

remainder of the weekend. It had been almost midnight when he'd got back to the house and she'd been in bed. There'd been no sign of her when he'd got up that morning either, although he hadn't lingered. He had skipped breakfast and come straight to the surgery, making do with a cup of coffee to tide him over. If he'd had his way he would have avoided seeing her for the rest of the day too, but obviously that wasn't to be. Now all he could hope was that the decision he'd made yesterday to behave calmly and professionally around her for the next couple of weeks would see him through.

'It has been busy,' she agreed evenly. Closing the door, she came over to his desk and handed him a file. 'Would you mind taking a look at this for me? I'm afraid it's got me stumped.'

'Of course.' Daniel took the file and quickly read through the patient's notes. His brows rose when he noted how many times the man had visited the surgery in the past two months. 'Alistair Grant is either an extremely sick man or he's a complete hypochondriac. You could fill a textbook with the variety of symptoms he's presented with recently.'

'Exactly.' She leant across the desk and selected a sheet from the file. 'Uncle Jim sent him for a whole battery of tests last month and they all came back clear.'

'Hmm.' Daniel placed the file on the desk, trying to ignore the leap his heart gave when her hand brushed his as she passed him the test results. Ruthlessly, he battened it down, refusing to allow himself even the tiniest leeway. He was going to treat Emma as a colleague from now on, even if it killed him!

'Does he seem genuine to you?' he asked, sticking determinedly to the matter under discussion.

'It's hard to say.' She grimaced. 'I only met him today so I don't have any real idea of what he's like as a person.'

'So he hasn't lived in Avondale all that long?'

'No. Apparently he moved here three months ago.'

'And almost immediately began visiting the surgery on a regular basis.' Daniel frowned as he picked up the patient's file again and flicked through it. 'How come we don't have any notes from his last GP?'

'He's been working abroad ever since he left university. He told me that he assumed his notes would be still at the practice his parents use but they've been unable to find them. Ruth has contacted the university to see if they were transferred to their medical centre but so far she's not heard back from them.'

'That's a shame. It would have been helpful to see if he had a history of visiting his GP on a frequent basis.'

'It would. To be honest, it's not a situation I've come across before. Most people who are undergoing surgery have been seen by several doctors before they reach us. That tends to weed out any malingerers.'

'Would it help if I had a word with him?' Daniel offered. 'I'm not saying I'll be able to tell if he's making it up, but it might deter him if he knows we're dubious about the claims he's been making.'

'Would you mind? I'd hate to make any hasty assumptions about his credibility and overlook something serious.'

Daniel heard the relief in her voice and immediately stood up. He would do anything to help her, he thought as he followed her to the door. He sighed as they walked along the corridor together. If only he'd thought about that on Saturday night. Making love with Emma may have been wonderful, but it had caused problems for him if not for her. She might be able to chalk it up to experience but he certainly couldn't. Just for a second his head reeled as he recalled how sweetly responsive she had been when he'd held her in his arms before he forced the thought to the deepest, darkest reaches of his mind. He couldn't afford to think about that or he wouldn't be able to function!

Alistair Grant was sitting in the chair exactly where Emma had left him. A thin young man in his late twenties with sandy-coloured hair and a pale complexion, he cut a rather pathetic figure. Emma smiled at him as she went into the room.

'I'm sorry to have left you sitting here, Alistair. This is Dr Kennedy. He would like to have a word with you to see if he can get to the root of your problems.'

'I hope somebody can.' Alistair stood up to shake hands. He sat down heavily again as though he didn't have the strength to remain on his feet for very long. Propping himself against the edge of the desk, Daniel regarded him thoughtfully.

'You seem to have been through the mill recently, Alistair. I've read your notes and you've had a lot of distressing symptoms in the last few months, it appears.'

Emma took her seat behind the desk, leaving

it up to Daniel to take the lead. She had to admit that the case had her stumped and she would value his help. She listened attentively while he asked Alistair how his health had been in general over the past year.

'I was fine right up until a few months ago,' Alistair assured them. 'I never had anything wrong with me before that apart from the odd cold.'

'Dr Roberts told me that you've been working abroad. Were you ill while you were there or did it all kick off when you came back to England?'

'When I moved to Avondale, actually. I'd only been here a couple of weeks when I started feeling really rough—tired and as though I had no energy. Then I started with all these aches and pains, the headaches, etcetera.'

He sounded really despondent and Emma frowned. If he was making it up then he was extremely convincing. By the time Daniel finished talking to him, she could tell that he was as perplexed as she was.

'I have to admit that it's got me baffled, Alistair. I know you've had a whole range of tests done, but I'd like to send you for more blood tests and see what they show up. Where were you working when you were abroad, by the way?'

'South Africa was the last place but I've been all over in the past few years—India, China, various parts of Africa. I'm a civil engineer so I go wherever the job takes me.'

'Are you working here at the moment?' Emma put in.

'Yes. I'm overseeing the building of a new wind farm. We're due to start in a couple of weeks' time so I've been doing a lot of the ground work beforehand.'

'I imagine there was opposition to building a wind farm around here,' Daniel suggested.

Alistair sighed. 'There was. It's taken years to get the go-ahead and there's a lot of folk who still aren't happy about it. One of the local farmers in particular has caused us a great deal of trouble—dumping loads of manure and old oil drums in the middle of the track to block our access, that sort of thing. Last week he even warned some of the men off with a shotgun. When we called the police, he claimed it was all a misunderstanding and that he was out shooting rabbits.'

'It can't be easy, dealing with that kind of behaviour!' Emma exclaimed.

'It isn't, although it wouldn't be so bad if I felt a bit more up to it,' Alistair stated ruefully.

'Well, let's hope we can get to the bottom of this as soon as possible,' Daniel said encouragingly. 'Bearing in mind where you've been working recently, I'd like you screened for some of the more obscure tropical diseases as well. It could be that you've picked something up overseas and that's what's causing the problem. We'll arrange for a blood sample to be sent to the School of Tropical Medicine in Liverpool and see if they can come up with any answers.'

Emma printed out a form for bloods to be taken

at the hospital, adding a request for samples to be sent straight to Liverpool. She handed the form to Alistair who thanked her rather wearily and left. She frowned as the door closed behind him. 'I don't think he's making it up, do you?'

'No. It didn't seem like it to me either,' Daniel agreed. 'Let's hope something shows up in the next lot of tests because it's very puzzling.'

'Fingers crossed.' She reached for the button to buzz through her next patient, not wanting to appear as though she was keen to detain him. However, he was way ahead of her.

'Let me know when the test results come back, will you?' he asked as he strode to the door.

'Of course.'

Emma summoned a smile but it was galling to know how eager he was to avoid spending any time with her. He had stayed away from the house all day on Sunday, only returning when he'd been sure that she would be in bed. She had heard his car turn into the drive well after mid-night and had hurriedly switched off her lamp, afraid that he would think she was waiting up for him.

It was obvious that Daniel was keen to avoid a repeat of what had happened on Saturday night. She was too but for a different reason. She was afraid of getting emotionally involved but that wasn't something he would worry about. Daniel simply didn't want any complications in his life. Maybe he *had* told her that she was more beautiful than any woman he had ever known but talk was cheap: actions said far more. And he had proved beyond any doubt that he didn't care a jot about her.

CHAPTER TEN

THE week wore on and Daniel found to his dismay that he couldn't stop thinking about what had happened between him and Emma. It wasn't so bad while he was working, he could focus on his patients then. However, when he was on his own, that was when the real problem started.

It was as though Emma had invaded his mind and every time he relaxed his guard, thoughts of her popped into his head. He kept remembering in glorious detail how it had felt when they'd made love and it was driving him mad. He longed to tell her how he felt yet he knew he couldn't do it. How could he confess that making love to her had touched his heart and his soul when it was clear that she didn't feel the same way?

In an effort to retain his sanity he spent an increasing amount of time away from the house. Fortunately the weather had improved and with the nights getting lighter, he was able to go walking after evening surgery ended. He became quite familiar with the various footpaths surrounding the town, although he was careful not to stray too far afield. It was while he was out one evening that he came across the search and rescue team tending an injured walker. When Mike Harding asked him if he would take a look at the woman's ankle, Daniel readily agreed.

'It looks to me very much like a Pott's fracture,' he declared after he'd examined her. He glanced at Mike and grimaced. 'When she fell, she broke her fibula and either broke the tibia as well or tore the ligaments, resulting in a dislocation of the ankle. It's a nasty injury.'

'Can you help us put a splint on it, Doc?' Mike asked. 'We certainly don't want to cause any more damage.'

'Of course.' Daniel gave the woman some

Entonox™ to help with the pain then helped Mike fit an inflatable splint to support her ankle. He accompanied the team back to their Land Rover, shaking his head when Mike thanked him profusely. 'I was happy to help.'

'I still appreciate what you did, Doc. That's twice in a very short time that we've been glad of your services. How's that young lad doing, by the way? Have you heard?'

'Do you mean Jack? He's been moved from Intensive Care and by all accounts is making an excellent recovery.'

'Which he probably wouldn't be doing if you hadn't been on hand to help him.' Mike shook his head when Daniel demurred. 'No, credit where it's due, Doc. You saved that kid's life and that's a fact. It's just a shame that you aren't going to be here long term. We could do with someone like you to call on, especially as we're coming up to our busiest time of the year. I don't suppose you'd consider moving here permanently, would you?'

'Nice idea, although I'm not sure my colleagues in London would appreciate me jumping ship,' Daniel told him with a laugh to disguise how touched he felt by the request.

'Pity. You've fitted in really well around here. Everyone's said so. And they don't always take kindly to outsiders, believe me.'

Mike sketched him a wave and drove off. Daniel made his way back to the house, thinking about what the other man had said. Despite the problems with Emma, he had enjoyed working in the town far more than he had expected. Not only had he enjoyed being part of such a close-knit community, he had dealt with a far wider variety of cases than he normally would have seen. With the nearest hospital being so far away, the surgery was the first port of call in an emergency and it had been good to test his skills.

He knew that if circumstances had been different, he would have been tempted to ask Jim Haynes if he was still interested in taking on a partner. There was certainly sufficient work for a second doctor; in fact, he couldn't imagine how Jim was going to cope on his own when he returned to work. However, he also knew how Emma would feel about the idea. He would be the last person she would want working here.

It was a dispiriting thought. Knowing how Emma felt about him hurt, even though he refused to examine the reasons why it was so painful. He knew that she would take care to ensure their paths never crossed in the future and it was hard to accept that once she left, he would never see her again. Even though he knew it was for the best, he was going to miss her.

Emma found it difficult to put what had happened between her and Daniel behind her. The fact that he never once alluded to it should have helped but it didn't. She found it deeply hurtful that he'd been able to dismiss the fact that they had slept together.

In an effort to make the remainder of her

stay in Avondale bearable, she made a point of keeping out of his way outside working hours. It wasn't difficult. Daniel had taken to going for a walk after evening surgery finished, which meant he was rarely at home. She did wonder if he was avoiding her too but decided she was being fanciful. Daniel had demonstrated very clearly that he had very few feelings for her, so why would he feel that he needed to keep out of her way?

Another week passed and the surgery was busier than ever. There was a steady influx of tourists arriving in the area and they added to the number of people wanting to be seen. Emma couldn't help wondering how her uncle was going to cope when he returned to work. Although he was making excellent progress, according to her aunt, running a busy practice with all that it entailed was very different from convalescing. She couldn't bear to think that Uncle Jim might put his health at risk out of a sense of duty and decided to speak to Daniel about it. She managed to catch him on his way out to some house calls on Friday lunchtime.

'Have you got a minute?'

'Yes, of course. What's up? Problems?'

He put his case on the desk and turned to face her. Emma felt her heart give a little jolt and swallowed. The weather had been exceptionally warm that day and he'd shed his jacket and rolled up his shirtsleeves. The pale blue cotton set off his olive-toned skin and provided the perfect foil for his dark brown hair. He looked big and vital and so gloriously male that she was suddenly aware of her own femininity in a way she hadn't been since the night they had made love.

The thought wasn't the least bit welcome. She hurriedly drove it from her mind and concentrated on what she'd come to say. 'I've been thinking about what's going to happen when Uncle Jim comes back to work.'

'You mean how he's going to manage on his own?' Daniel said immediately, and she looked at him in surprise.

'Yes. How did you know that's what I meant?'

'Because I've been thinking about it too.' He gave her a tight smile. 'It doesn't take a genius to see that he's going to be pushed to keep up with the workload here. Quite frankly, it's way too much for one person.'

'It is. He needs someone to help him, ideally another partner, but I can't see that happening, can you?'

'It could take time to find the right person,' Daniel said slowly. 'And it isn't something we can organise without your uncle's consent.'

'No, it isn't. And if Uncle Jim is as choosy this time round as he was the last time he advertised, it could take for ever.' She sighed. 'It's hard to know what to do, isn't it?'

'How about a locum?' Daniel suggested.

'Do you think we'd find anyone willing to work here, though?'

'I can't see why not. Oh, I know Avondale isn't exactly a mecca for bright lights and a wild social life, but neither is it the back of beyond.

And at this time of the year—when the weather is fine—it might be an attractive proposition for someone.'

'It's worth a try,' she said slowly. 'I don't suppose you know any reliable agencies who provide locum cover? It's not something I've had to deal with.'

'I'll get onto our practice manager and ask her for some phone numbers,' Daniel assured her. 'We often need locum cover so she keeps a list of agencies.'

'That would be great. Thank you. Should we tell Uncle Jim what we're planning when he phones?'

'Oh, yes, I think so, don't you?' He shrugged. 'If I were in his shoes, I'd expect to be kept up to date with what was going on here.'

'I only hope he doesn't object,' Emma said anxiously. 'You know how touchy he can be about his patients, wants to be sure they receive first-class care, et cetera.'

'Leave it to me. I'm sure I can convince him

it will be in everyone's best interests if he has help, if only during the summer months.'

'That's probably the best way to sell the idea to him,' Emma agreed. 'Even Uncle Jim will have to admit that it's hard to cope when there are so many visitors in the area.'

'And once he's admitted that, it should be easier to make him see that he needs help at other times of the year as well.'

'Take it one step at a time, you mean?' she said, frowning as she considered the idea and realised that it had a lot of merit.

'Yes.' Daniel sighed. 'Trying to push your uncle into admitting that he isn't up to running the practice on his own any longer will only make him dig in his heels, so we'll take things slowly, let him discover for himself that he needs help.'

'It makes sense. I'd hate it to look as though we doubt his capabilities.'

'Exactly. This way, any decisions that are made about the future of the practice will be his. He won't feel as though he's being pushed into doing something he doesn't want to do.'

'You're right,' Emma agreed, surprised by Daniel's astute assessment of the situation. She knew that her uncle would hate to feel as though he wasn't in charge any more, but it surprised her that Daniel had realised that too.

She turned to leave then stopped when Daniel said suddenly, 'Oh, by the way, those test results for Alistair Grant have come back. I was in the office when they arrived so I had a look at them. I hope you don't mind?'

'Of course not. What did they show? Anything?'

'According to the lab at Liverpool there are traces of pesticide in Alistair's blood.' Daniel shrugged. 'It would certainly explain the wide variety of symptoms he's presented with recently, wouldn't it?'

'It would. Do you think he's been in contact with pesticides while he's been here or did it happen while he was working overseas?' she queried.

'Liverpool seems to think the problem is recent. I've asked Ruth to phone Alistair and get him to make an appointment to see if we can find out how he may have come into contact with the chemicals. If we can't find an answer, I imagine environmental services will need to be alerted to see if they can sort it out.'

'Of course. If it is a local problem then we don't want anyone else being taken ill,' she said worriedly.

'Exactly.' He smiled at her. 'I'll mention it to your uncle when he phones. I'm sure he'd enjoy getting to the bottom of the mystery.'

'I'm sure he would,' she agreed quietly.

Emma sighed as she left the room. She couldn't help wondering how one person could be such a contradiction. On the one hand Daniel genuinely seemed to care about other people's feelings, but on the other hand he didn't seem to care a jot about hers. Even though she knew it was stupid, she couldn't help wishing that he would spare some of that concern for her.

The house calls had taken far longer than he'd expected so that it was after three p.m. by the time Daniel drew up in front of Niths Farm. He switched off the engine and reached for the printout that Ruth had prepared for him. According to the patient's notes, it had been over ten years since Harold Dawson had last visited the surgery. He'd suffered an injury to his left arm following an incident with some kind of farm machinery but had refused to go to the hospital. Jim had stitched his arm, given him a tetanus shot, and that had been it. Harold Dawson hadn't returned to have the stitches removed and had ignored several telephone messages asking him to contact the surgery. Daniel grimaced as he got out of the car. It didn't bode well for what was going to greet him today.

He rapped on the farmhouse door, glancing around while he waited. Although the farm was large, it was very untidy. Bits of rusty old machinery littered the yard and there was a pile of stones heaped up in the corner where one of the barn walls had given way. The whole place had a pervading air of neglect that saddened him. It seemed a shame that what had been once an obviously thriving concern should have been reduced to such a pitiful state as this.

'Aye? And what do you want?'

Daniel swung round when a gruff voice spoke behind him. He summoned a smile as he greeted the elderly man standing in the doorway. 'I'm Dr Kennedy. You phoned the surgery and requested a home visit.'

'I asked to see the real doctor, not some stand-in,' the man replied rudely. He glared at Daniel. 'Tell them I want to see Dr Haynes, no one else.'

'I'm afraid Dr Haynes is away at the present time,' Daniel explained quietly.

'Then I'll wait till he's back.'

He went to shut the door but Daniel put out his hand and stopped him. 'Dr Haynes won't be back for another month. Are you sure you want to wait that long, Mr Dawson?'

The man hesitated while he considered the idea. He scowled as he wrenched open the door. 'Suppose you'd better come in, then, seeing as you're here.'

Daniel sighed ruefully as he followed the old man into a dingy hallway. Not exactly the warmest welcome he'd ever received. Harold Dawson led him down the hall to the kitchen, which turned out to be equally neglected. Daniel's heart sank as he took stock of the piles of dirty dishes on the draining board and the inch-thick layer of grease that coated the top of the old-fashioned range. It didn't appear as though any cleaning had been done in the place for months, if not years. Pushing aside a stack of old newspapers, he placed his case on the table.

'So what exactly is the problem, Mr Dawson? You told Ruth it was something to do with your foot, I believe.'

'That's right, although I wouldn't have bothered phoning if I weren't in so much pain.' The man glared at him. 'I don't hold with all these pills you doctors hand out. Don't do folk no good, in my opinion.'

Daniel forbore to say anything, deeming it wiser not to get embroiled in an argument he was unlikely to win. 'I'd better take a look at your foot.'

Harold Dawson sat down heavily on a chair and started to peel off a filthy sock from his right foot. Daniel shook his head in dismay when he saw the how red and swollen it looked.

'When did this start?' he asked, kneeling down in front of the old man.

'A few weeks ago, mebbe a bit longer,' Harold replied curtly. He winced when Daniel touched the inflamed skin. 'It's real tender so don't you go poking and prodding at it.'

'I'll be as careful as I can,' Daniel assured him. He carefully felt the swollen foot, pausing when he discovered a strong pulse beating beneath the flesh because it confirmed his initial diagnosis.

Standing up, he took a bottle of hand gel out of his case, deeming it more hygienic than using the sink to wash his hands.

'It looks to me as though you have immersion foot, Mr Dawson. It's a type of injury caused when feet are allowed to remain wet and cold for a prolonged period. You may have heard of trench foot which so many soldiers in the First World War suffered from? It's the same thing.'

'I've not been standing in any trenches,' Harold retorted scathingly.

'I'm sure you haven't. But if you've been outdoors and got your feet wet and not bothered to change your shoes and socks, that could have caused it.' Daniel tactfully didn't add that from the state of the man's socks there was no *could* about it. It was doubtful if Harold Dawson had put on clean socks or anything else for a very long time!

He took a prescription pad out of his case and wrote out a script for painkillers. 'I imagine your foot's very painful so these will help. You'll also need to bathe your foot in tepid water to cool it and reduce the swelling. Make sure you put on clean, dry socks and that your shoes or boots are dry too.' Daniel handed the man the prescription. 'If you notice any sores appearing, contact the surgery. Skin ulcers can develop and that's something we want to avoid.'

'So that's it, is it?' Harold Dawson slammed the prescription down on the table. 'Take some pills and put on dry socks. I could've worked that out for myself!'

Daniel smiled calmly, resisting the urge to tell the man that if he'd done that in the beginning there wouldn't have been a problem. 'That's right. It's just a question of taking care of yourself.'

'I don't need any advice from you,' the old man responded belligerently. He shuffled towards the door, making it clear that he expected Daniel to leave.

Daniel picked up his case, knowing how pointless it was to suggest that he arranged for the community nurse to call and check how Harold's foot was healing. If the poor woman received the kind of reception he'd received, she would probably refuse to call a second time, and he wouldn't blame her either. He made a note to speak to Ruth about the old man when he got back to the surgery and headed out to the hall, pausing when there was a loud banging on the front door.

'What the dickens…!' Harold Dawson pushed past him and strode along the hall. Wrenching open the door, he glowered at the young man standing outside. 'You can take yourself off my property right now.'

'Believe me, I'd like nothing better than not to see hide nor hair of you or this place for the rest of my life,' the other man retorted.

Daniel frowned when he realised that the caller was Alistair Grant. It seemed a coincidence that he should turn up here when he needed to speak to him. However, he was less concerned about resolving Alistair's health issues at that moment than he was about defusing the situation.

He hurried to the door, hoping to avert a full-scale row.

'Hello, Alistair,' he said quietly, drawing both men's attention to him. 'I'm surprised to see you here.'

'I'm not here out of choice, believe me, Dr Kennedy,' Alistair replied angrily. He glared at the old man. 'If you don't stop dumping stuff on the road to the construction site then I warn you, Dawson, that the company I work for will take legal action. Carry on with your little games and you'll find yourself in prison. Is that clear?'

'Aye, it's clear enough. But if you think a young pup like you can come to my home and threaten me, think again.'

Daniel's heart sank when he saw Harold Dawson reach behind the front door and pick up a shotgun that had been standing there. He aimed it at Alistair Grant's chest. 'You need to learn some manners, lad, and I'm just the one to teach them to you.'

'Come on, now, let's all calm down,' Daniel said soothingly. He stepped forward then stopped when Dawson swung round and pointed the gun at him.

'I've told you once that I don't need any advice from you.' The old man scowled at him. 'You're no better than he is. Coming in here, thinking you can tell folk what to do. Well, I've had enough, do you hear me? It's 'bout time someone stood up to the likes of you. Inside, both of you.'

Dawson waved the shotgun towards the kitchen. Daniel hesitated but one glance at the old man's face warned him that it would be foolish to refuse to do what he asked. He headed back along the hall, wondering what was going to happen next. Maybe Dawson only wanted to scare them but he didn't think so—it looked far more serious than that.

He put his case on the table as Alistair followed him into the room, seeing the sheen of perspiration on the younger man's face. It was obvious that he was scared stiff and Daniel didn't blame him. Harold Dawson was on the brink of losing control and there was no knowing what would happen then.

A picture of Emma suddenly appeared in his mind's eye and he felt a shaft of regret so sharp run through him that he winced. He couldn't bear to think that he might die without telling Emma that he loved her.

CHAPTER ELEVEN

'I DON'T suppose you've seen Daniel, have you, Emma?'

Emma paused when Ruth called to her on her way into the surgery that afternoon. It was five minutes to four and she was keen to get to her room before her first patient arrived. 'Not since lunchtime, I'm afraid.'

'Oh, right.' Ruth sighed.

Emma frowned. 'Why? Is there a problem?'

'No, not really. It's just that he usually pops in with his notes after he's finished the house calls, but he's not been in yet this afternoon.'

'Maybe he's running late,' Emma suggested.

'Probably, although there weren't that many calls to do today.' Ruth shrugged when the phone rang. 'Maybe he got held up. You know how some people love to talk—he probably couldn't get away.'

'I expect that's it,' Emma agreed as she carried on along the corridor, although she was surprised that Daniel would have allowed himself to be late. He was a stickler for punctuality and was usually at his desk well before his first appointment was due.

She booted up her computer then glanced through the list that Ruth had left on her desk. It wasn't too long for a change so, hopefully, she could finish on time for once. She buzzed through for her first patient, smiling when Judith Fisher walked into the room.

'Hello, Judith. How are you?'

'I'm all right, Dr Roberts.' The young woman sat down in front of the desk. 'I had an appointment at the hospital on Wednesday. The consultant did a laparoscopy and confirmed that I have endometriosis, like you suspected.'

'At least we know what we're dealing with now,' Emma said quietly.

'I suppose so,' Judith agreed wistfully.

Emma guessed that it had been a blow for Judith to have her suspicions confirmed and tried to focus on the positive aspects of the diagnosis. 'What did the consultant suggest by way of treatment?'

'He's put me back on the Pill to prevent me menstruating. It will help to control the pain and, hopefully, stop the cysts from getting any bigger. He also said that he might surgically remove some of the larger cysts at a later date.'

'And you're worried about how that will affect your chances of having a baby?'

'Yes.' Tears rose in Judith's eyes. 'I don't think I'll ever have a baby now, will I?'

'I haven't received a copy of your consultant's report yet, Judith, so there is no way that I can tell you that everything is going to be all right. However, what I can say is that between sixty and seventy per cent of women who suffer from endometriosis are able to have children.'

'That sounds much better than how the consultant put it.' Judith managed a watery smile. 'He said that thirty to forty per cent of women with endometriosis are infertile.'

'I suppose it's the glass half full or half empty scenario,' Emma said with a chuckle. 'It depends which way you choose to look at the figures.'

'Well, I prefer your way.' Judith sounded more optimistic all of a sudden. 'I have almost a seventy per cent chance of becoming a mum and that's pretty good odds, I'd say.'

'So would I.' Emma smiled at her. 'I know it must be hard but try to remain positive. Once you've completed the treatment, who knows what might happen? And the plus factor is that pregnancy is known to suppress the symptoms of endometriosis.'

'A case of fingers crossed.' Judith laughed as she stood up.

'Exactly.'

Emma was still smiling as she buzzed through her next patient. It was always good to know that you had helped someone be more positive about their life. That was one of the reasons why she loved surgery, of course, although she hadn't realised that she would derive the same pleasure from general practice work. No wonder Daniel enjoyed his job so much.

The thought startled her. Ever since Daniel had announced that he planned to go into private practice, she'd had a jaundiced view of his motives for becoming a GP. Now she could see that she may have misjudged him. It didn't necessarily mean that it was purely financial gain that drove him.

It was uncomfortable to find her view of Daniel knocked off kilter. Emma found it difficult to push the idea aside as she dealt with her next patient, an elderly man who suffered from chronic bronchitis. She renewed his prescription for an inhaler and gently suggested that he might benefit from oxygen therapy. Once she had explained that oxygen cylinders could be delivered to his home, he happily agreed. She made a note to ask Ruth to contact the nearest supplier and saw him out. She was just about to sit down again when Ruth, herself, hurried into the room.

'I'm sorry to barge in, Emma, but Daniel still hasn't appeared. I'm getting really worried now, because it just isn't like him not to turn up,' the receptionist told her anxiously.

'No, it certainly isn't,' Emma agreed. 'Have you tried his phone?'

'Yes, but it goes straight to voice mail.' Ruth bit her lip. 'You don't think he's had an accident, do you? Some of the roads round here are a bit tricky if you don't know them that well.'

'I'm sure we'd have heard if he had,' Emma assured her, although her heart had started to race at the thought of Daniel lying injured somewhere. She took a deep breath before panic could set in. 'Do you have a list of the calls he was supposed to do this afternoon?' When Ruth nodded, she hurried on. 'Then I suggest you telephone everyone on the list and check what time he visited them. That way we'll have a better idea of where he might be.'

'Good idea!' Ruth exclaimed. She hurried to the door then paused. 'What about his patients, though? There's a real backlog forming.'

'I'll have to see them,' Emma told her. 'I'll see one of mine then one of Daniel's—that will be fairer than making his patients wait till I finish my list.'

Emma picked up the phone as soon as Ruth left and dialled Daniel's phone but the call went straight to voice mail again. She hung up, feeling her stomach churning with nerves. What could have happened to stop him even answering his phone? She had no idea but it was extremely worrying. Maybe they didn't see eye to eye on a lot of things but she couldn't bear to think that he may have been hurt or worse even.

Her heart suddenly seemed to shrivel up inside her. The thought of never seeing Daniel again was more than she could bear.

* * *

Daniel heard his phone ring and guessed that it must be Ruth calling to see where he was. He glanced at his watch, realising with a start that it was almost four-thirty. How much longer was Dawson going to keep them here? he wondered, glancing at the old man, who was standing guard by the kitchen door. He had no idea but something needed to be done to resolve this situation soon.

'Look, Mr Dawson, I know you're upset but this is crazy. Keeping us here won't achieve anything,' he said in his most reasonable tone. 'All you'll do is find yourself in a whole load of trouble and I'm sure that isn't what any of us wants.'

'I don't care how much trouble I'm in. It'll be worth it to put a stop to what's going on.' Harold Dawson raised the shotgun and pointed it at Alistair Grant. 'If him and his cronies think they can come here and tear up the countryside then they can think again!'

Daniel saw the colour drain from Alistair's face

and quickly interceded. 'If that's the way you feel, you need to talk to someone, see if you can get the decision to build this wind farm reversed.'

'Talk! I've talked till I'm blue in the face and no one's listened to me.' Harold's face flushed with anger. 'No, it's actions that will get their attention, nothing else.'

Daniel opened his mouth to try again to make him see sense when the telephone rang. Harold Dawson lifted the receiver off its rest. Daniel could tell from what the old man was saying that it was the surgery phoning and guessed that Ruth must be checking up on his whereabouts. He was tempted to shout out that he was there but Dawson must have realised he might do that and swung the gun towards him.

'No, the doctor left a while ago. No, I don't know what time it was. I've better things to do than keep a check on folk's comings and goings.'

He went to slam the receiver back on its rest at the same moment that Daniel's mobile phone rang again. He let it go to voice mail once more, knowing it would be foolish to try and answer it. Dawson's mood was far too volatile to risk upsetting him any further. He glanced at Alistair and saw the fear in the younger man's eyes.

'What are we going to do?' Alistair mouthed desperately.

Daniel shook his head. Reasoning with the old man obviously wasn't going to work and using physical force was out of the question when Dawson had that gun. All he could hope was that Emma would call the police when he failed to turn up. So long as she didn't try tracking him down herself, of course.

The air seemed to lock in his lungs at the thought of her following him to the farm and placing herself in danger. He knew if that happened he would have to do something, no matter how risky it was.

He took a deep breath and his mind was suddenly crystal clear. He would give up his life to protect Emma because he loved her.

* * *

It was seven o'clock before the last patient left. Emma hurried through to Reception, not needing to ask if there was any news when she saw the worry on Ruth's face. 'Still nothing,' she said helplessly.

'No. I just don't know what to do next, Emma.'

'You've called everyone who'd requested a home visit?'

'Yes, and they all said that Dr Kennedy had left ages ago.' Ruth shook her head. 'Most of them were able to tell me almost to the minute what time he left too. It was only old Harold Dawson who refused to say what time Daniel left his farm but that's typical of him. A really awkward old devil, he is.'

'Harold Dawson from Niths Farm, you mean?' Emma queried.

'That's right. He's always been difficult but he's got worse since his wife died. He doesn't have any family and I doubt he's got any friends either…' Ruth paused and frowned.

'What?' Emma said quickly. 'You've obviously thought of something.'

'It's just that when I was hanging up the phone after speaking to him I could have sworn I heard a mobile phone ringing in the background.' Ruth shrugged. 'It just seems odd. I wouldn't have thought old Mr Dawson would be the sort to bother having a mobile.'

'Maybe he had somebody visiting him,' Emma suggested.

'Could be, although I doubt they'd get much of a welcome. He's not one to mix, believe me.'

Emma sighed. Although it did seem strange, it had nothing to do with what had happened to Daniel so there wasn't time to worry about it right then. She came to a swift decision. 'I'm going to phone the police and report Daniel missing. I'm not sure what they can do but we can't just sit here, wondering what's happened to him.'

'I think you should call them,' Ruth agreed, looking relieved. 'Daniel would have let us know if his car had broken down or if he'd had some sort of minor accident.'

Emma bit her lip as she reached for the receiver. Ruth was right. Daniel *would* have contacted them—if he could. She put a call through to the police station and told them what had happened. They promised to check with the various agencies in case Daniel had been involved in an RTA and get back to her. Ruth insisted on staying while they waited for the police to phone back and went off to make them a cup of tea. Almost as soon as she'd gone, there was a loud banging on the surgery door and Emma felt her spirits soar in relief. That had to be Daniel!

Hurrying to the door, she swung it open. 'And about time too—' she began, then stopped abruptly when she found Mike Harding standing on the step. 'Sorry, Mike. I thought you were someone else.'

Mike grimaced. 'And I'm sorry to turn up like this too but I noticed the lights were still on as I was passing.' He held up his hand, which was covered in a blood-soaked bandage. 'We've been out on a training exercise tonight and I managed to get my thumb caught in one of the ratchets we use to haul people up the hillside. It needs a stitch or two and I was hoping you might do it to save me having to trail off to the hospital.'

'I…um…yes, of course. Come in.' Emma led the way inside. 'Come straight through to my room while I take a look at it.'

Mike followed her along the corridor, glancing round when Ruth came rushing out of the staff-room. He must have seen her face fall because he grinned. 'Obviously, I'm not the person you hoped to see either.'

'No, you're not,' Ruth said bluntly.

Mike's smile faded as he looked from her to Emma. 'Is something wrong?'

'Daniel failed to turn up for surgery this evening,' Emma explained as she ushered him into her room. 'He hasn't phoned and he isn't answering his mobile either.'

'That's odd.' Mike frowned as he sat down and

unwound the bandage. 'I wouldn't have thought there was a problem getting a signal in that part of the Dales.'

Emma stopped and stared at him. 'What do you mean, that part of the Dales? Have you seen him?'

'Yes, well not *him* but I've seen his car. It's parked outside old man Dawson's place—Niths Farm. You know.'

'What time was this?' Emma demanded.

'Oh, around six-thirty, give or take a few minutes.' Mike shrugged. 'I did my hand in soon after that so it can't have been much later.'

'But Ruth phoned Harold Dawson way before then and he told her that Daniel had already left!' Emma exclaimed.

'Well, it was definitely Dr Kennedy's car. You don't get many fancy motors like that round here and certainly not at Dawson's place. There was another car there too, now that I think about it, a site vehicle from that wind farm they're building on the edge of Dawson's land.' Mike looked worried now. 'Why on earth did Dawson say the doc wasn't there when he was?'

'I don't know but it needs checking.' Emma picked up a dish and filled it with saline then gently bathed Mike's thumb. She frowned when she saw the deep gash at its base. 'That looks nasty. It's going to need three or four stitches by the look of it.'

She numbed Mike's thumb with an injection of local anaesthetic then set to work. It only took her only a few minutes to complete the job and Mike shook his head in admiration. 'That was quick work. You've done that a time or two, by the look of it.'

'Just a couple of times.' Emma summoned a smile but it was hard to concentrate. She had a nasty feeling about what Mike had told her and wouldn't rest until she had paid Harold Dawson a visit to see what was going on.

'Dr Haynes told me that you'd gone into surgery.' Mike smiled at her as he stood up. 'He's every right to be proud of you.'

Emma merely nodded, her mind too busy churning over possibilities to focus on the compliment. She looked up when Mike sighed. 'If it's hurting I can give you some painkillers,' she offered, feeling guilty for neglecting her patient.

'It's fine. No, it's obvious that you're worried sick about Dr Kennedy, aren't you?'

Emma flushed. 'It just seems strange that he hasn't called us,' she demurred.

Mike gave her an old-fashioned look. 'Hmm. It does. Why don't we drive over there and see what's going on? It's the least I can do after you've saved me a long wait in Casualty.'

'Oh, I couldn't expect you to do that,' she began, but Mike shook his head.

'Of course you can. In fact, I'm going to get onto the rest of the team and tell them what's happened. If the doc's out there, we'll find him. That's a promise.'

He put a comforting arm around Emma's shoulders and she sagged gratefully against him. 'Thanks, Mike,' she murmured huskily.

'No sweat.' He gave her a brotherly hug then went to the door. 'I'll put through that call and see you outside. OK?'

Emma nodded then hurried to find Ruth and tell her what had happened. They agreed that the police should be informed that Daniel's car had been seen, although whether they would act on the information was open to question. Mike had the engine running when Emma hurried outside and as soon as she got into the Land Rover, they set off. It was a good thirty-minute drive to Niths Farm and Emma was on tenterhooks all the way. If Daniel had left the farm, she had no idea where to start looking for him.

They turned down the lane leading to the farm and Mike slowed as they reached the bottom. 'Look,' he said, pointing.

Emma's heart leapt into her throat when she saw Daniel's car parked in the yard alongside another vehicle, which bore the logo of the wind farm's contractors. Obviously he was still there despite Harold Dawson's assurances to the contrary. 'What should we do?' she asked anxiously.

'I don't know, but whatever we decide we need to be careful.' Mike's tone was sombre. 'Old Dawson is a bit of a loose cannon lately. Folk have seen him walking round with a shotgun. Let's not go rushing in until we know what's happening, eh?'

'But Daniel may be in danger!' she protested.

'Yes. And we don't want to make matters worse by forcing Dawson's hand.' Mike picked up the radio receiver. 'I'm going to call the police and get them over here right away.'

Emma opened her door and climbed out of the car while Mike made the call. There were only a few hundred yards between her and Daniel but the distance had never seemed greater. The fact that she had no idea what was happening to him was so painful that she felt tears well to her eyes. Maybe they weren't destined to spend their lives together, as she had once hoped, but that didn't matter. So long as she knew that he was safe and well somewhere in the world, that was enough. In that moment she was forced to acknowledge the truth. She loved him. She loved him with the whole of her heart and she always would.

CHAPTER TWELVE

DANIEL heard the sound of a car stopping in the lane and frowned. Was it possible that someone had come looking for him and Alistair? He glanced at Harold Dawson but the old man seemed oblivious to what was happening outside. Dawson had grown increasingly agitated in the past hour. He had placed the shotgun by the back door and started walking around the kitchen, muttering to himself. Daniel might have been tempted to make a grab for the shotgun if it weren't for the fact that someone could get hurt if there was a struggle. It had seemed safer to bide his time but he might not have that luxury for much longer. He turned to Alistair.

'There's a car stopped in the lane,' he mouthed.

'Do you think it's the police?' Alistair whispered, hopefully.

Before Daniel could answer, Harold Dawson swung round and glared at them. 'Don't you two start thinking you can get up to anything.' He grabbed hold of the shotgun and pointed it at them. 'I won't think twice about using this, I warn you.'

'And what will that achieve, Mr Dawson?' Daniel said in sudden exasperation. 'You'll end up in prison and the wind farm will still go ahead.'

'At least they'll know they can't trample all over me,' Harold roared. He aimed the gun at the ceiling and pulled the trigger. Daniel ducked as bits of wood and plaster rained down on them. His ears were throbbing from the noise of the explosion so that it was several seconds before he could hear let alone speak.

'Force isn't the answer,' he told the old man grimly. 'The powers-that-be won't give in because you threaten them. You need to go through the proper channels.'

If Dawson was listening he gave no sign of it. Daniel realised that he was wasting his breath trying to reason with him. He glanced towards the window, mentally crossing his fingers that it was the police outside and not some other unsuspecting visitor. His heart turned over at the thought that it might be Emma before he realised how foolish it was to imagine she cared enough to try and find him. Emma may have contacted the police when he hadn't turned up for evening surgery but that would have been all. She certainly wouldn't be spending her time worrying about him.

Emma's heart seemed to stop when she heard the sound of a shotgun being discharged. Mike was speaking to the police on the radio and she saw the shock on his face as he looked up. He hastily finished his call and hung up.

'The police will be here ASAP,' he told her.

'They said that we're not to approach the house and that under no circumstances are we to try and contact either Dawson or Dr Kennedy.'

'But we can't just sit here,' Emma protested. 'Anything could be going on inside that farm-house. We need to do something!'

'We daren't risk it, Emma. I know it's hard but we could make matters a whole lot worse if we go rushing in.' Mike patted her hand. 'Let's wait for the police, love. They know what they're doing.'

Emma bit her lip. She knew Mike was right but it was sheer agony to wonder if Daniel might be hurt. It seemed to take for ever before the police arrived. She and Mike told them everything they knew, which was very little. When the police insisted that they back up the lane, she protested, but the police were adamant. They couldn't risk there being any civilian casualties.

The time dragged after that. The police used a loudhailer to speak to Harold Dawson, trying to persuade him to let the hostages go. He refused all their pleas, ending the negotiations by firing the shotgun out of the window. Armed police officers were deployed to surround the house and everyone looked very tense. However, by the time midnight arrived, little progress had been made.

Emma couldn't imagine what it must be like for Daniel and the other hostage being caught up in such a drama. All she could do was hope that Harold Dawson would come to his senses and let them go. And if he did then she intended to tell Daniel the truth about how she felt. She loved him and she wasn't going to lie about it, wasn't going to pretend any more. She would tell him the truth—and hope that it meant something to him.

Daniel could feel his nerves humming with tension. Ever since Dawson had fired that shot at the police, he had become increasingly unstable. Daniel knew that he was within a hairsbreadth of losing control and had no idea what would happen then. Somehow he had to get the old man talking and hopefully defuse the situation.

'Why exactly are you so against this wind farm being built?' he asked as Harold made another circuit of the room.

'Because it shouldn't be there, that's why.' Harold glowered at him but Daniel tried not to let it deter him.

'You think it will spoil the countryside?'

''Course it will. Who wants to look at dozens of great lumps of metal? My Mary wouldn't. That's for sure.'

'Mary's your wife?' Daniel said quickly, wanting to keep the conversation flowing.

'Was. She died six years ago.' Tears suddenly welled into the old man's eyes. 'She loved the view over those hills, did my Mary. There's a meadow there that's full of wildflowers in the spring and she always said it was the most beautiful place on God's earth. Even when she was so ill that she couldn't get out of bed most days, she'd ask me to take her up there. And now folks like him want to dig it all up and spoil it.'

He jerked his thumb at Alistair, who blanched. Daniel realised that he had hit upon the real crux of the problem. Harold Dawson's desire to stop the wind farm going ahead was all tied up with his late wife. He realised that he needed to tread warily.

'No wonder you're upset about what's happening,' he said quietly. 'It must be difficult to accept that a place which meant so much to your wife is going to change. But do you think Mary would have been happy about what you're doing?'

'What do you mean?' Dawson demanded querulously.

'Keeping us here and threatening us. Shooting at the police.' Daniel shrugged. 'What would Mary say if she knew that was what you were up to?'

Harold Dawson stopped pacing; his expression was reflective. 'My Mary hated guns. She wouldn't even let me shoot rabbits when she was alive. Said it was cruel, she did.'

'Then I doubt if she'd have approved of this, would she?' Daniel held out his hand. 'Why not give me the shotgun, Mr Dawson. Let's stop this now before things get any worse.'

Harold Dawson hesitated then slowly handed over the shotgun. Daniel carefully ejected the cartridges then placed it against the wall and stood up. 'I suggest we tell the police that we're coming out.'

Dawson didn't try to stop them as he and Alistair walked along the hall. Daniel cautiously opened the front door, shouting out that he and Alistair were coming out. Everything happened at great speed after that. The police came running towards them, some of the officers going straight into the house while others hurried him and Alistair away to safety. People were firing questions at him from all directions and he did his best to answer them, but he had caught sight of a figure standing just beyond the police cordon. Emma was here? She had cared enough to come and find him?

His heart sang with joy as he walked straight past the policeman who was trying to speak to him. Emma had started walking too, ducking under the tape, so that they met in the middle of the lane. When he opened his arms, she stepped into them and it was then that he knew everything was going to be all right. How could it not be when the love of his life was here in his arms, her heart beating in time with his?

He bent and kissed her, uncaring that everyone was watching them. He didn't give a damn who knew how he felt so long as Emma knew it. Drawing back, he looked into her eyes, wanting there to be no more misunderstandings, either deliberate or accidental.

'I love you,' he said softly, his voice grating with emotion. He felt the tremor that ran through her, heard the sharp indrawn breath she took, and held her tighter, knowing it must be a shock for her to hear him say that. He had hurt her so much, seemingly thrown away her love, and it was a lot to ask her to believe him now, but he had to try. 'I love you, Emma. I always have.'

'Daniel, I…'

She stopped and swallowed. Daniel could see the uncertainty in her eyes and prayed that she would find it in her heart to give him another chance. He wanted to take her somewhere quiet and explain it all to her, but there was no hope of that right now. He sighed when the officer in charge came over and told him firmly that he needed to speak to him at the police station. It appeared that sorting things out with Emma would have to wait for now.

'I'll have to go,' he told her huskily, smoothing a silky lock of her hair behind her ear. He dropped a kiss on her lips then smiled at her. 'I'll be back as soon as I can. Will you wait up for me?'

'Yes.' She gave him a wobbly smile, her eyes holding his fast for a moment before she turned away.

Daniel watched her walk over to Mike, who put a friendly arm around her shoulders as he led her to his car. He would have felt better if they could have sorted things out immediately rather than wait, but there was nothing he could do. As he allowed the officer to lead him to the waiting police car he sent up a silent prayer that everything would be all right. He just needed Emma to give him a second chance.

It was five a.m. before Emma heard a car turn into the drive. She ran to the window, feeling her heart leap when she saw Daniel getting out of a police car. Hurrying into the hall, she flung open the front door, seeing the lines that fatigue had been etched onto his handsome face.

'I thought they were never going to let me go,' he said as he stepped into the hall. 'I must have gone over what happened a dozen times before they were satisfied that I'd told them everything.'

'Come into the sitting room.'

Emma led the way, waiting until he had sunk

down onto a chair before she went back to the door. She had spent the intervening time wondering what would happen when he got back. He had told her that he loved her but was it true? She longed to know yet now that the moment had arrived, she was suddenly afraid. What if Daniel hadn't really meant it, what if it had been merely a reaction to the stress he'd been under? She wasn't sure if she could cope with the disappointment of having her hopes dashed a second time.

'I'll make you a drink,' she said hurriedly. 'What do you prefer—tea or coffee?'

'Neither, thank you. My stomach is awash with the foul brew that passes for tea at the police station.' He gave her a gentle smile as he held out his hand. 'Come and sit down, Emma. We need to talk.'

Emma bit her lip as she slowly sat down on the end of the sofa. She didn't know how she was going to bear it if Daniel told her it had been the stress of the moment that had made him say that he loved her. People said all sorts of things they didn't mean when they were under pressure, after all.

'Emma, about what I said before—' he began, but she didn't let him finish, couldn't bear to hear him say the words that once again would rip open her heart.

'I understand, Daniel. Really I do.' She gave a light laugh and saw him frown.

'You do?'

'Of course. You were under a huge amount of strain. It's perfectly understandable if you…well, if you said something you didn't really mean.'

'So you think that I didn't mean it when I said that I loved you?'

His tone was so devoid of expression that Emma found it impossible to guess what he was thinking. She shrugged, not wanting him to suspect how difficult this was for her. She loved him so much, had even planned to tell him that, but now she realised how foolish it would be. She simply couldn't bear to put herself in the position of having her heart broken all over again.

'I think it's perfectly natural that you reacted to the stress of the moment. People say the strangest things when they're under pressure.'

'I see. And you're not angry that I said what I did?'

'Of course not! We've all said things we've regretted, Daniel. It's part and parcel of being human, so please don't worry about it.'

'It's kind of you to take that view,' he said gruffly.

Emma frowned when she heard the roughness in his voice. He sounded upset but why should he be when she had offered him the perfect escape route? It was very strange but before she could work out what might be wrong, he stood up.

'I think I'll try and snatch a couple of hours' sleep or I'll be fit for nothing.'

He left the room before Emma could stop him. She followed him into the hall but he had already gone upstairs. She made her way to her room and lay down on the bed, fully clothed. She had done the right thing, she assured herself, given Daniel the let-out he'd needed. He didn't love her and it would have been a mistake to let herself believe that he did. Tears trickled down her cheeks but she didn't try to stop them. She needed to cry out all the disappointment and put it behind her if she was to get on with her life.

The sound of the door suddenly opening made her jump. Pushing herself up against the pillows, she stared at Daniel in surprise. 'Daniel! What is it?'

'I'm probably about to make a complete and utter fool of myself but there is no way that I can let this go.' He came over to the bed and glared down at her. 'I didn't tell you that I loved you because I was under pressure, Emma—far from it. For the first time in a long while I was thinking clearly. Letting you go five years ago was the hardest thing I have ever done. Not a day has passed since then when I haven't wished that I could have done things differently. I love you, Emma. That's the plain and simple truth. It might not be what you want to hear but it's what I need to tell you.'

He spun round on his heel and strode out of the door but there was no way that Emma was prepared to let him leave after making such a mind-blowing statement. She scrambled off the bed and ran after him, catching up with him on the landing. 'Daniel, wait! You can't come barging into my room and tell me that and then just…*storm* back out!'

'Better I do that than commit another sin,' he ground out, his eyes blazing into hers in a way that made a shaft of heat sear through her.

Emma felt her breath catch when she saw the expression in his eyes. It wasn't anger that had driven him to such extremes of emotion, she realised, but desire, desire for *her*. Her hand half lifted in a gesture that could have been interpreted either way, as a rejection or as an invitation. Even she wasn't sure what it meant, but then Daniel took a step towards her so that she could feel the heat of his body burning into hers, and her mind was suddenly crystal clear. She wanted him. Only him.

Her arms wound around his neck at the same moment as he reached out and hauled her towards him so that their bodies collided with a small thud, as though they had been struck by a mini-earthquake. Emma could feel the aftershocks rippling through her, tiny flurries of sensation that made her feel wonderfully alive. As her fingers buried themselves in the crisp dark hair at the nape of Daniel's neck, she murmured softly—sounds, not words—because forming anything as difficult as a word was beyond her, but Daniel seemed to understand what she meant anyway.

His mouth found hers, his lips parting hers so that he could plunder her mouth, and she groaned. There was nothing gentle about the kiss, nothing tender. It was as though every scrap of raw passion had been distilled into this one kiss, so that she was breathless when it ended, her body throbbing, her mind numb, her heart awash with emotions.

'Emma, my sweet, sweet Emma.'

His voice was hoarse as he gently laid her down on the carpet and started to undo the buttons down the front of her shirt. Emma would have loved to help him but her hands wouldn't respond. They were locked around his neck, her fingers still buried in his cool crisp hair, and they refused to let go. She just lay there as he finished unbuttoning her shirt and parted the edges, lay there still as he reached beneath her and unclipped her bra. It was only when he lifted her right breast free of the lacy cup that the spell was broken and she was able to move but even then her hands remained locked around his neck as she drew his head down, inviting him to suckle her.

She gasped as a wave of intense pleasure rushed through her when his lips closed around her nipple. There was no slow build-up of passion, no need for caresses or time. She wanted him, right there, right now, this minute.

He lifted his head and must have seen how she felt because he shuddered. Emma could feel the tension in his body as he stripped off her clothes then shed his own. He made love to her there on the floor, his body pressing hers down into the carpet, but even though everything was heat and passion, there was tenderness, too. And it was that more than anything else that convinced her that Daniel had been telling her the truth. He did love her. Her heart soared at the thought.

Daniel could feel his heart pounding as he slowly came back down to earth. Making love with Emma had always been the most wonderful of experiences and this time they had reached new heights. Propping himself up on his elbows, he stared down into her face, feeling his love for her swamp him.

'Wow! I'm not sure how that came about but

it was definitely something else,' he murmured, buzzing her lips with a kiss.

'It was.' She smiled as she cupped his cheek with her hand. 'A definite wow in my book too.'

'I'm glad to hear it.' Daniel laughed throatily. 'At least I don't have to apologise for not finding somewhere more comfortable.'

'Oh, it's comfy enough.' She wriggled a little and his breath caught when he felt her body moving beneath his. Even though it was only moments since they had made love, he could feel himself responding. 'Although I may need to check my backside for carpet burns.'

'If you do find any, I'll be more than happy to administer a little first aid,' he assured her, grinning.

'I'll let you know,' she told him, laughing.

Daniel kissed her lightly on the mouth then rolled to his feet. Although he could have happily stayed there all day, they needed to talk and they couldn't do it there. He offered her his hand, unable to resist pulling her into his arms when she stood up.

'I didn't plan for that to happen, Emma, but I'm glad that it did.' He raised her chin so that he could look into her eyes. 'I know you think that I was under a lot of pressure earlier but I'm not under any pressure now and I still feel the same. I love you and that's why I made love to you just now. I only hope that somehow, some way, I can make you believe me.'

'I do believe you, Daniel.' She gave a little shrug when he gasped. 'You couldn't have made love to me like that and not cared.'

'No, I couldn't,' he agreed, his heart overflowing with emotion. He kissed her on the lips then led her to her room and gently steered her through the door. 'We need to talk and I won't be able to concentrate if you're in that state of undress. Put something on and come downstairs. We'll talk then.'

She didn't say anything as she went into her room and closed the door. Daniel went back to his own room and quickly dressed, hoping he hadn't made a mistake by suggesting they waited. Would Emma start to have second thoughts while she was away from him? He hoped not but even if she did, he would convince her that he was telling her the truth. What would happen then was up to her, of course, and his stomach sank at the thought that his future was hanging in the balance. He might love Emma with his whole heart and every fibre of his being, but he had no real idea how she felt about him.

CHAPTER THIRTEEN

EMMA could feel her stomach churning as she made her way down the stairs. Now that the rush of euphoria had started to fade, she'd had time to think and there were a lot of questions that needed answering, the main one being that if Daniel had loved her five years ago then why had he let her go? Maybe he had been keen to further his career but surely he must have known that she would have supported him? After all, she had offered to give up her own dreams of becoming a surgeon so they could be together—how much more proof had he needed about her commitment to him? It was all very puzzling so it was little wonder her heart was racing as she went into the sitting room.

'That was quick.'

He stood up and came over to her, taking her hand to lead her over to the sofa. He had switched on the gas fire and the room felt warm, too warm, in fact. Emma sank down onto the cushion, feeling slightly faint, although maybe it was the ambiguity of the situation that was causing her to feel like this rather than the temperature. She needed answers and she needed them now.

'Look, Daniel, I…'

'I know how difficult…'

They both spoke at once and both stopped. Emma bit her lip in an agony of frustration. They would get nowhere if they carried on this way.

'You first.' Daniel sat back in his seat and regarded her gravely. 'What were you going to say?'

'Just that I don't understand why you pushed me away if you loved me, as you claim to have done.'

'The simple answer is that I was afraid,' he said quietly.

'Afraid?' Emma looked at him in confusion. 'What of?'

'Of hurting you. Of ruining your life.' He stared down at the floor for a moment and his expression was bleak when he looked up. 'Of you ending up hating me.'

Emma didn't know what to say. She stared at him in silence, too shocked by the statement to dispute it. Daniel sighed heavily as he reached for her hand and linked his fingers through hers.

'I decided it was better if I drove you away rather than run the risk of that happening, Emma. Maybe I was wrong but I did it with the best of intentions. I did it for you and I hope you will believe that.'

'It's hard,' she said shakily. 'You hurt me so much, Daniel. At the time I didn't know if I would ever get over what you'd done, and now you tell me that you did it for me—'

She broke off, unable to disguise her scepticism. She hated to think that he might be lying to her but what else could she think? She had offered him her love and he had rejected it in the cruellest way possible. How could that have been to her advantage?

She went to stand up, not sure if she could sit there and listen to any more, but he pulled her back down beside him. His tone was urgent now, the look he gave her filled with desperation.

'I'm not explaining this very well, so it's no wonder that you're confused. But what I said was true. Sending you away seemed like the only thing I could do to protect you.'

'Protect me? From what? I loved you, Daniel. I wanted to be with you and told you that. Surely you must have known I was telling you the truth?'

'Of course I did!' He gripped her hand so hard that she winced and he swore softly, under his breath, as he released her. Standing up, he went over to the window and stood there, staring out across the garden. And when he spoke his voice echoed with so much pain that it brought tears to her eyes.

'I knew you loved me, Emma, and that was what scared me, the fact that you loved me so much you were willing to give up your dreams to be with me.' He turned and she could see the regret in his eyes. 'I couldn't let you do that, my darling. It was too great a risk, you see.'

'No, I don't see. I don't understand what you mean, Daniel.' She leant forward beseechingly. 'I would have been happy to give up my plans to become a surgeon if it had meant we could be together.'

'I know you mean that but can't you see that it would have driven a wedge between us eventually?' He came back and knelt in front of her. 'You admitted only the other day that you would have regretted giving up surgery, so how long do you think it would have been before you'd blamed me for making that decision?'

She started to demur but he shook his head. 'No, I've seen it happen before, Emma. It was the reason why my own parents' marriage failed. My mother was just starting out as a barrister when she met my father. He was in the diplomatic service, which meant he was posted overseas for long periods of time. It would have been impossible for Mum to pursue her career after they married so she gave up the law.'

'But surely she must have thought it all through, weighed up the pros and cons before she made her decision?'

'Of course she did, and I suppose she thought that being with Dad was more important than anything else.' He shrugged. 'Sadly, it didn't work out that way. Mum became increasingly resentful about giving up her career. My childhood was one long round of arguments about it, in fact. It was a relief when I was sent to boarding school because it meant I didn't have to listen to my parents fighting.'

'It must have been horrible for you,' she said quietly, and he shrugged.

'It wasn't a happy time. Mum was bored and

frustrated, and Dad felt guilty because if it hadn't been for him, her life would have been very different. The sad thing was that they really loved one another in the beginning but it wasn't enough.'

'And you believe it wouldn't have been enough for us either?' Emma said flatly.

'No, I don't think it would have been. I think that in time you'd have regretted giving up so much for me.' He squeezed her fingers. 'I knew how much surgery meant to you, you see. That's why I discounted the idea of moving to Scotland to be with you while you did your training.'

'You would have done that for me?'

'Yes, willingly, if it had been the right thing to do. The problem was that I knew you would need to devote all your time and energy to your work. Surgery isn't an easy option and I would have been an unnecessary distraction.' He sighed. 'That's why I told you that my career meant more to me than our relationship. I wanted to protect you, Emma, and, if I'm honest, I wanted to protect myself as well. I couldn't have stood it if one day I'd seen resentment in your eyes when you looked at me because you'd failed to achieve your ambitions.'

Daniel took a deep breath. He had no idea how Emma was going to react to what he had told her and the strain made him feel as though every nerve had been stretched to breaking point. He literally jumped when she finally spoke.

'Why didn't you tell me all this, about your parents and everything, five years ago?'

He looked up but it was impossible to guess what she was thinking and his nerves seemed to tighten that bit more. 'Because I was afraid that you would persuade me that none of it mattered, that what had happened to my parents would never happen to us,' he told her simply.

'Maybe it wouldn't have done. Maybe we could have worked things out somehow. The trouble is that you weren't prepared to give us a chance, were you?'

'I wasn't prepared to take any risks,' he corrected, his heart sinking when he heard the bitterness in her voice.

'But it wasn't just your decision, Daniel. It was mine too, only I wasn't allowed to decide what *I* wanted. You took things out of my hands and that was it.' She stood up abruptly. 'Maybe I can't say for certain that our relationship would have lasted, but I would have liked the chance to try and make it work. You denied me that opportunity and no matter how well intentioned your motives were, you didn't have the right to do that. You didn't trust me, Daniel. That's what it all boils down to. And that hurts more than anything else.'

She left the room and Daniel heard her footsteps walking along the hall. He wanted to go after her and beg her to believe that he had done it for her benefit but he knew how pointless it would be. She needed time to come to terms with what he had told her, time to work out how she felt about him now that she knew the truth.

He put his head in his hands as a wave of despair washed over him. He had to face the fact that Emma might not be able to forgive him for what he had done. He might lose her again for telling her the truth, just as he had lost her before for trying to protect her.

It was a busy morning. As well as having to deal with an exceptionally long list, Emma was summoned to the police station at lunchtime to make a statement about what had happened the previous evening.

She stuck determinedly to the facts. How she had felt when she'd realised that Daniel was missing wasn't the issue and the police didn't need to know about that. However, when she left the station an hour later she felt both physically and emotionally drained. Recalling the moments when she'd thought Daniel had been hurt had brought back all the horror.

She made her way to the nearest coffee shop and sat down at a table, wondering what she was going to do. She loved Daniel so much, but discovering that he hadn't trusted her to know her own mind five years ago hurt unbearably. The fact that he had chosen to end their relationship rather than try to make it work made her wonder if he really understood what love meant. Maybe he'd thought he'd loved her then as he thought he loved her now, but did he? Really? Was he even capable of the depth of love she felt for him?

By the time she left the coffee shop, her head was throbbing from trying to work it all out. It had started to rain heavily and the traffic was moving at a snail's pace as she drove through the town. Emma grimaced as she glanced at the dashboard clock. She was going to be late for evening surgery if she didn't get a move on.

She managed to pick up speed once she left the town. There were a lot of cars on the road, probably visitors to the area who were driving around to avoid getting soaked. She overtook a car and caravan combination then had to slow down again when she found herself stuck behind a tractor. The road was too narrow to overtake and she had to wait until it turned off before she could put her foot down. She crested the bridge over the river and breathed a sigh of relief. Just another couple of miles and she'd be home.

The thought had barely crossed her mind when she felt the car suddenly skid when the tyres hit a patch of mud lying on the road. Turning the wheel, she tried to correct the sideways movement but to no avail. There was a horrible scrunch of metal as the car hit the side of the bridge, followed by a loud bang as the driver's airbag exploded. The noise was deafening so that it was several minutes before Emma realised that someone was knocking on the side window. The man gestured for her to unlock the door, which she did.

'Are you all right?' he demanded, bending so he could peer into the car.

'I think so.' She tentatively tried moving her arms and legs. 'Yes. Everything seems to be working OK.'

'What about your neck?' he said quickly when

she went to unbuckle her seat belt. 'You can't be too careful when it comes to neck injuries. That's what they say on the television, how you should always make sure a person's neck is properly supported. Maybe you should sit there until the ambulance arrives in case you do yourself any damage.'

'Oh, but I don't need an ambulance,' she protested. 'I'm fine, really.'

'Best to make sure,' the man insisted. 'Anyhow, I've phoned them now so it would be silly not to let them check you over.'

Emma sighed. She could hardly refuse to let the paramedics treat her, seeing as they'd been summoned. She dug her phone out of her pocket and called the surgery, briefly explaining to Ruth what had happened and that she would be back as soon as possible. She had just finished when the ambulance arrived so she turned off her phone while she answered the crew's questions.

They examined her thoroughly, checking how

her pupils responded to light and making sure that she hadn't been unconscious at any point before finally agreeing to let her get out of the car. The driver's door was jammed against the wall so she had to slide over to the passenger seat to get out and was surprised to find how shaky she felt when she stood up. The accident had caused quite a long tailback of traffic on both sides of the bridge, too. Emma grimaced as she turned to one of the paramedics.

'I seem to have created havoc,' she began, then stopped when she spotted a figure running towards them. Her eyes widened in shock when she realised it was Daniel.

'What are you doing here?' she began, but he didn't let her finish. Sweeping her into his arms, he stared down into her face and she was stunned to see the fear in his eyes.

'Are you all right, Emma?'

'I'm fine,' she told him shakily.

'Are you sure?' He glanced at her car and she

saw the colour leach from his face when he saw the state it was in.

'Quite sure. Aren't I, guys?' She glanced at the paramedics, who added their endorsement to her claim. Daniel took a deep breath and she felt him shudder.

'Thank heavens for that. When Ruth told me you'd been in an accident…'

He couldn't go on but she understood. He'd been as terrified about her as she'd been about him the night before. All of a sudden the doubts she'd had melted away. Daniel loved her, he really and truly did. It was the most glorious feeling to know it for certain once more.

Reaching up, she kissed him lightly on the lips. It was no more than a token but she could tell he understood what it meant when she saw his eyes blaze with joy. Emma could feel the same sense of happiness and wonderment bubbling inside her as they thanked the ambulance crew. A couple of the other drivers helped Daniel push her car off the road so that the traffic could start moving again. Once that was done, Daniel phoned the local garage and arranged for the car to be collected.

'That's it, then. Let's get you home.' He put his arm around her waist as he led her back to where he had left his car part way up the lane. Emma slid into the passenger seat, smiling as he bent and dropped a kiss on her lips.

'Mmm, what have I done to deserve that?' she teased.

'Nothing. Everything.' He kissed her again then closed the door and walked round to the driver's side. He started the engine then turned to look at her. 'I love you, Emma. I know you were hurt this morning when I told you why I had ended our relationship. I did what I thought was right, although now I can see that I shouldn't have made the decision all by myself. I just hope that one day you can find it in your heart to forgive me.'

'There's nothing to forgive. You were trying to protect me, Daniel, because you loved me.'

'Yes, I was. Maybe I went about it the wrong way but it was the only way I could think of at the time.' He took her hand and raised it to his lips. 'You meant the world to me then, Emma, just as you mean everything to me now.'

'And you mean the world to me, too, so let's not waste any more time.' She leant over and kissed him softly on the cheek. 'From now on any decisions about our future shall be made together. Agreed?'

'Agreed!'

He gave a whoop of laughter as he planted a kiss on her mouth then put the car into gear. They headed back to the surgery and it felt to Emma as though they were floating on a cloud of happiness rather than doing anything as mundane as driving. Daniel refused to let her help him take evening surgery and dispatched her straight to the house with orders to put her feet up until he got back. Emma didn't protest because she wasn't sure she was in a fit state to be seeing patients while she was functioning at this level of euphoria.

She let herself into the house and waited for Daniel to return, knowing what would happen when he did, and it was just as she had expected. They made love to each other with a joy and intensity that brought tears to both their eyes.

'I love you, my sweet Emma,' Daniel told her as he held her against his heart. 'I want to be with you for ever, if you'll let me.'

'It's what I want too,' she told him honestly. 'Although I'm not sure about the logistics of it, with you working in London and me in Scotland.'

'Trivialities,' he assured her airily. 'We have far more important things to worry about, like when we're getting married.'

'Married?' She sat up straight and stared at him. *'Married!'*

'Uh-huh.' He pulled her back into his arms and kissed her slowly, grinning wickedly when he heard her moan. 'That's what couples do when they're in love. They get married and live happily ever after.'

'So this is a proposal, is it?' she said when she could summon enough breath to speak.

'I suppose it is.' He suddenly rolled to his feet and knelt by the side of the bed, smiling up at her as he took her hand. 'I'd better do it properly so there's no mistake. Will you, Emma Roberts, do me the honour of becoming my wife?'

'Yes,' she whispered then repeated it much louder so there would be no mistake about her answer either. 'Yes, I will!'

EPILOGUE

Three months later...

EMMA stepped in front of the mirror and studied her reflection. It was her wedding day and she wanted everything to be perfect, even though it had been a rush to get things organised in such a short space of time. Now she smiled as she took stock of the dress she had chosen.

Made from pure silk in the palest shade of cream, it fell in soft folds to the floor. The cream rosebuds that the hairdresser had pinned into her hair that morning exactly matched the colour of the fabric. More rosebuds had been hand-tied to form a posy which she would carry up the aisle. She knew she looked her best and hoped that Daniel would think so too. They had waited so long for this day to come and she wanted it to be special, a celebration of their love for each other.

A knock on the bedroom door heralded the arrival of her aunt. Both her aunt and her uncle had been thrilled when she and Daniel had announced that they were getting married. It appeared that they had known all along how she had felt about Daniel five years ago. Although he would never admit it, Emma suspected that her uncle had been doing a bit of matchmaking when he had asked Daniel to cover for him.

It had been Uncle Jim who had suggested that Daniel should think about becoming a partner in the practice, an offer which Daniel had eagerly accepted, much to Emma's delight. It had solved the problem of where they should live as once they returned from honeymoon, she would be taking up a new surgical post at the local hospital. She and Daniel would start their married life in Avondale, where they had first met and fallen in love.

'Your uncle sent me upstairs to check if you were ready,' her aunt informed her, taking a tissue out of her bag. 'You look beautiful, Emma, really beautiful.'

'Thank you.' Emma gave her aunt a hug then smiled at her. 'Shall we go? I don't want to keep Daniel waiting.'

There was quite a crowd gathered outside the local church when they drew up a short time later. Emma smiled when she spotted Alistair Grant, who was acting as one of the ushers. The source of his problems had been traced to the old chemical drums Harold Dawson had used to block access to the wind farm. Environmental services had visited Niths Farm and removed a number of other drums containing hazardous liquids. It was good to know that the community she was going to be a part of once more was no longer at risk.

The organist struck up 'The Wedding March' as they stepped inside the porch and her uncle gave her hand a reassuring squeeze. 'All set, my dear?'

'Yes.'

Emma took a deep breath as they set off down the aisle but the moment she saw Daniel waiting in front of the altar her nerves disappeared. Here was the man she loved, the man she wanted to spend her life with. From this moment on they would be together for ever.

Daniel felt his heart turn over as he watched Emma walking towards him. It was as though every hope and dream he'd ever had had crystallised into this one moment. She stopped beside him and he saw the love in her eyes when she turned to look at him and knew she could see the same emotion in his. They loved each other. They trusted each other. They were meant to be together.

Taking her hand, he made himself a promise that no matter what happened in the future nothing would spoil what they had. Maybe he had been afraid in the past but he wasn't afraid any longer. He loved Emma and she loved him. They had everything they needed to guarantee a wonderful life together.

* * * * *

January

THE PLAYBOY OF HARLEY STREET	Anne Fraser
DOCTOR ON THE RED CARPET	Anne Fraser
JUST ONE LAST NIGHT…	Amy Andrews
SUDDENLY SINGLE SOPHIE	Leonie Knight
THE DOCTOR & THE RUNAWAY HEIRESS	Marion Lennox
THE SURGEON SHE NEVER FORGOT	Melanie Milburne

February

CAREER GIRL IN THE COUNTRY	Fiona Lowe
THE DOCTOR'S REASON TO STAY	Dianne Drake
WEDDING ON THE BABY WARD	Lucy Clark
SPECIAL CARE BABY MIRACLE	Lucy Clark
THE TORTURED REBEL	Alison Roberts
DATING DR DELICIOUS	Laura Iding

March

CORT MASON – DR DELECTABLE	Carol Marinelli
SURVIVAL GUIDE TO DATING YOUR BOSS	Fiona McArthur
RETURN OF THE MAVERICK	Sue MacKay
IT STARTED WITH A PREGNANCY	Scarlet Wilson
ITALIAN DOCTOR, NO STRINGS ATTACHED	Kate Hardy
MIRACLE TIMES TWO	Josie Metcalfe

April

BREAKING HER NO-DATES RULE	Emily Forbes
WAKING UP WITH DR OFF-LIMITS	Amy Andrews
TEMPTED BY DR DAISY	Caroline Anderson
THE FIANCÉE HE CAN'T FORGET	Caroline Anderson
A COTSWOLD CHRISTMAS BRIDE	Joanna Neil
ALL SHE WANTS FOR CHRISTMAS	Annie Claydon

May

THE CHILD WHO RESCUED CHRISTMAS	Jessica Matthews
FIREFIGHTER WITH A FROZEN HEART	Dianne Drake
MISTLETOE, MIDWIFE...MIRACLE BABY	Anne Fraser
HOW TO SAVE A MARRIAGE IN A MILLION	Leonie Knight
SWALLOWBROOK'S WINTER BRIDE	Abigail Gordon
DYNAMITE DOC OR CHRISTMAS DAD?	Marion Lennox

June

NEW DOC IN TOWN	Meredith Webber
ORPHAN UNDER THE CHRISTMAS TREE	Meredith Webber
THE NIGHT BEFORE CHRISTMAS	Alison Roberts
ONCE A GOOD GIRL...	Wendy S. Marcus
SURGEON IN A WEDDING DRESS	Sue MacKay
THE BOY WHO MADE THEM LOVE AGAIN	Scarlet Wilson

1211 LP 2P P2 Me